The DELICIOUS FLOWERS

A Myrtle Jenson Mystery

M. MALENGA

The following is a work of fiction. Any names, characters, places, and incidents are the product of the author's imagination and are entirely fictitious. Any resemblance to actual persons, living or dead, is entirely coincidental.

ISBN-978-1-7345744-5-6

DEDICATION

Mother.
Sisters.
Brother.
Father.

"Doing something you love is a fortunate way to live" ~ Myrtle Jenson

THE DELICIOUS FLOWERS

A Myrtle Jenson Mystery

CHAPTER 1

It was an ordinary evening when a naked man fell
through the ceiling. The body is discovered dead and
surrounded by a sea of broken glass shards from the
glass ceiling he had crashed through. Some things
cannot be unseen. Years later without warning her
mind will still drift back to that night. Over time she
has learned to cope with it. She blocks it out and
refocuses her mind on being present. Breathing
exercises reconnect her to her immediate
surroundings and she starts to feel better already.
Presently the guest of honor is making his way to the
podium to begin his remarks.

"The swirl of clouds is a wonderous thing that
enticed us all."

Professor Weatherford delights the crowd by reading
excerpts from his new memoir. Tonight, is an evening

to celebrate award-winning literature. The dinner guests have gathered to celebrate the English Professor and the release of his new book. There is also a silent auction after the dinner to raise money for the English Department at the local University. The venue for the dinner party is the Professor's stately manor. The home was built in the late 1800s and was at one time the grandest home in Viewgrove. A deep recession forced the original owners to abandon the property and over time it fell into disrepair. There was debate around town about possibly converting the property into a government building, but that never materialized. The manor went unoccupied until 10 years ago when Professor Weatherford purchased it and began restoring the property to its former glory. The Professor does not live in the manor. Most of the town residents are curious to view the renovated manner, however this event is invitation only and that includes a few select press members. The expectation is the Professor will autograph a few books for guests. The title of the book is 'The Magic of the Beginning'. Professor Weatherford reads about how he and his childhood friends would spend lazy summer afternoons staring at clouds in the English countryside where he grew up. As children, they found great joy in daydreaming about the future and describing all the different things they saw in the clouds. The crowd hangs on every word and applauds loudly when he is done.

Denise is so excited to attend this event. The room is filled with the who's who of Viewgrove. She loves this high society pomp and circumstance stuff. To top things off, she was seated at a table next to Fannie Dubai. The Dubai family owns several prominent businesses around town. They also have a wing in the local hospital named after them. Fannie qualifies as high society in Viewgrove and moves in those exclusive circles. The local tabloid paper nicknamed her 'Fancy Dubai' because of the extravagant designer clothes and jewelry she wears around town. If you did not know who she was you would think she had just stepped off stage from performing at a rock concert. Her wardrobe resembles more of a costume than a designer collection. "It costs money to look that tacky", the tabloids would often write. The tabloid writers would be correct, these designer garments and flashy jewelry are not cheap by any means. Fannie Dubai has been dressing this way for so long that nobody can remember back to a time when she did not. Now that she is a senior people simply accept it as Fannie just being Fannie, it is how she is most comfortable presenting herself.

Denise is seated at the table letting all the ambiance wash over her. She is tempted to take out her phone and take pictures, but she fears that may be frowned upon. Looking around she does not see anybody else with a phone out. The first course the waiters bring out is the salad. This is no ordinary salad; this is a masterpiece to behold. The salad resembles more of a garden. There is a wide range of greens and edible flowers forming a bright array of colors and textures. Denise reckons this is a salute to tonight's honoree and his time spent as a youth in those English meadows. In front of the salads is a small carafe of Honey Lime Vinaigrette to dress the salad. Off in the near distance is a beautifully decorated cake that follows the theme of the night. It resembles the winning entry on a televised professional baking challenge show, three tiers flawlessly wrapped in white fondant. The cake is decorated with the most inornate red, yellow, and blue frosting flowers piped out of royal icing. Each dinner table is elegantly set with eight formal place settings surrounding a crystal centerpiece. The chandelier light dances around the design intricacies in the table centerpiece and creates a sparkling effect. Whoever decorated the room appears to have thought of every detail. Denise does her best to hide her excitement, she feels like she is on one of those royal British shows that she loves so much. Now looking at the formal table setting it appears all her years of watching period piece television shows are about to pay off. The table setting resembles something out of an English movie with a variety of cutlery and glasses to choose from. Denise is not intimidated in the least and knows immediately to use the outermost fork to her left to start the first course.

She is proud of herself for remembering that detail.

The noise level in the room lowers as people start to enjoy their garden salads. Soft classical music fills the air as the live band plays. The murmur of private conversations mixes seamlessly with the sound of salad forks clinking against fine China. There is a rumble at the table as a dropped fork clanks loudly off a plate. A drinking glass is knocked over spilling water onto the salad plate, table, and floor. The other guests at Denise's table look over to find her clutching her chest and gasping to breathe. The color is leaving her face. One of them yells for somebody to help, "She's choking!" Just as quickly as it had started the gasping stops and her eyes glaze over. "I know CPR!" A young waitress runs over to perform the Heimlich maneuver, arriving just in time to witness what happens next. With a thud, Denise's limp body falls face-first onto the table, right next to her $500 per plate salad. A startled Fannie screams at the top of her lungs. Now more guests from other tables start to look toward the source of the screaming. The young waitress positions herself behind Denise and lifts her to her feet. Once in position, the waitress frantically works to dislodge the blockage. To her dismay, she can feel Denise's body fall limp, there is no response.

"AIYEEEEE, she's dead, somebody, do something!", screams Fannie Dubai.

CHAPTER 2

It has been months since anybody has been murdered in Viewgrove. This is wonderful news unless you are in the criminal murder solving business. With no murders to investigate, Myrtle Jenson must find other ways to spend her time. Before agreeing to become a Police Consultant with the Viewgrove PD, she had dreams of spending her retirement reading on the beach. Up until now, she has not had time to read in her retirement but now, she did. Unwinding in a beach chair with a good book by the water is one of her favorite ways to pass the time. Admittingly, she has not been reading a lot of award-winning literature lately. Viewgrove or VG as the locals call it is not bordered by an ocean. However, it does have a lake with a decent size beach that Myrtle likes to frequent. It is not an ocean view, but the beach sand is clean, and the lake water is not polluted with trash. Myrtle is almost positive this is a man-made lake and beach, probably created to increase commerce and trade at some point in the town's development. The beach is a popular hangout for younger residents. The younger residents nicknamed the town View Grave because of all the older people that move there to retire. The new school year has begun, so the children are back in school and not crowding the beach. With her beach chair and umbrella now set-up, she reaches into her beach bag and retrieves a novella she has been reading. The sun shines on her brown skin, warming the parts of her legs that are not covered by the shade of the umbrella.

A novella is a fictional story somewhere between a short story and a novel in length. Myrtle has become obsessed with them in the last few months and buys them on sight whenever she comes across a novella she has not read. They have become her secret vice. Her favorite place to shop for these short books is the train station gift shop. The book selection is smaller so the limited selection forces her to make a quicker purchase decision than whenever she visits the local bookstore. She always loses track of time in the bookstore and almost always spends way more money than she intends to. What she enjoys about novellas the most is there is not a large time commitment involved. These types of books fit easily into a busy retiree's schedule. They are perfect for reading by the pool while on vacation, on train rides home, or on a sunny beach. Myrtle reads for enjoyment and hates to think about how many books she read through the end only because she had invested so much time reading it. Even if a novella is bad, it does not feel like such a waste because the end is not far away. As is the example with the book Myrtle is reading right now. It is not especially interesting so at times she finds herself taking a page count to see how much of the book is left to go. After the last few months, anything will do to get her mind thinking about something else besides not working. The crime-solving consulting work she does with the Police is extremely rewarding and it is an adrenaline rush that is hard to replace. The book is a mystery novel about a murder that takes place in a small town. "How cliché", thought Myrtle when she initially read the back-cover description in the train station gift shop. Over the years she has learned to never discount a book based on its cover. She strongly believes that wonderful things can be found in unexpected places so long as you are open to looking.

The lake waves produce a soothing sound as they wash up on the beach. A cooler evening breeze blows over the beachgoers signaling the shift from afternoon to evening. It is a summer night, so it is still light well into the evening. The sun begins to set splashing vibrant hues of red, yellow, and orange across the distant horizon. Sunsets put Myrtle in a reflective mood. Something about the sunset colors calms her down and conjures up memories of her deceased husband and the retirement plans they made. Once painful memories, they now bring her comfort. They were to retire together and travel the world sharing sunsets in exotic locations. His murder changed all of that, it changed everything. Myrtle's life was on a different path, a path that was interrupted and forever changed. That event motivated her to dedicate her life to the pursuit of justice. His murder is the reason she ends up in Viewgrove and eventually working with the Police as a consultant. The cell phone buried in Myrtle's beach bag begins to ring. It takes a minute for her mind to even register the phone is ringing. The sound is like an alarm clock going off in the morning or a familiar voice reminding her it is time to go. Five more minutes, she would love to stay in this moment for five more minutes, but she cannot. The moment is lost, and she is back in the present. Myrtle marks her progress by placing her laminated bookmark between the off-white book pages. A short rummage through her beach bag and she locates her cell phone before it stops ringing.

"Hello, this is Myrtle."

CHAPTER 3

Within minutes of the 911 call being placed, the
Viewgrove Emergency response team is on the scene.
The venue's parking lot is lit up with the glow of
flashing lights from the ambulance and firetruck. The
paramedics part the small crowd of people huddled
around a body. In the center of the crowd, they find
Denise laying on the floor next to her chair and
unresponsive. One of the waiters has been trying to
give her CPR. The paramedic immediately takes over
the Cardiopulmonary Resuscitation (CPR) in a valiant
effort to revive her. Unfortunately, all attempts to
revive her are unsuccessful. The mood in the room
quickly turns from hopeful to solemn. The lead
examiner asks if anybody knows what happened.
After hearing several accounts of the events leading,
the lead emergency response officer calls the Police.
Minutes later there are red and blue Police lights

adding to the light show in the parking lot. First through the door is Detective Casper 'Zeus' Chaplin, sporting an olive trench coat and a tan fedora hat.

"What do we have here?"

The lead emergency response officer rushes over to brief him on the situation. Zeus sighs deeply, even a grand event like this is unable to shield itself from the unspeakable.

Myrtle arrives at the mansion to find Detective Zeus Chaplin is already on the scene. Party guests are giving their statements to officers, and others that have been released are waiting for the valet to bring their cars around. Due to the emergency response vehicles upfront, Myrtle parks her car behind the valet line and walks up to the front door. The police officer securing the scene recognizes her and lets her through. Myrtle is a little nervous being on a crime scene again, it has been a few months since she has done this. She immediately locates Detective Chaplin and heads toward him. He is easy to find as his 6'4" frame towers over most everybody present. This tall dark handsome man would not go unnoticed in most crowds. Myrtle has no doubt he was extremely popular with the ladies in his younger days, probably still is.

"It's good to see you again Zeus."

"Thanks for coming down so quickly, it's good to see you too."

Myrtle plays it cool, but it truly is good to see Zeus again, she missed him. She is unsure what the appropriate form of greeting is after being apart so long, do they shake hands, wave, or maybe hug? It turns out to be none of those, but it is good to feel needed again.

Zeus Chaplin quickly explains to Myrtle how there was a death at the gala. The eyewitnesses report the victim choked to death. The lead emergency response officer feels the victim's pupils and skin coloration are not consistent with what you expect to see from a choking death. The first response paramedic reached into the victim's throat and found no blockage; however, the blockage could be further down the victim's throat. The lead emergency response officer believes the victim could have also had a violent allergic reaction to something she ate. An autopsy will tell investigators the exact cause of death.

"Detective, you called me in for a choking accident?"

The emergency response believes the victim may have choked on her food; however, they cannot say definitively. The emergency response teams in Viewgrove are trained to veer on the side of caution when it comes to deaths. In the event they missed something, and it was anything but an accident they want to be able to say they did their due diligence. The recent rash of lawsuits against city police departments for mishandling investigations is enough to make any police department take notice.

"The high-profile nature of this case is why I called you in, Ms. Jenson."

The victim's body is laying under a sheet on the medical team's gurney waiting to be released by Detective Chaplin. Myrtle lifts the sheet to examine the body and her heart drops when she discovers her friend Denise is the victim. She had forgotten all about receiving an invitation to this event. She feels so guilty because she now remembers giving Denise her invitation months ago. Myrtle hates these formal types of events, but she knew Denise loved them and would get so much more out of going than she ever could. Who would want to kill Denise, she did not even know most of these people? Just then an awful thought comes to mind, is somebody perhaps trying to kill her, but has mistakenly killed Denise? The thought makes her shudder and she instantly fights to push it out of her mind. Zeus, the constant detective, is observant enough to recognize the change in Myrtle's mood. Although she tries to disguise it, her sudden grief is on clear display on her face. Detective Chaplin is frozen, this reaction is unexpected and for a moment he is at a loss for words.

"Did you know her?"

The simple answer is yes, but that does not even begin to properly answer the question. Denise is one of the first real friends she made in town. It was a rain-soaked morning in May when she ventured out in search of a coffee shop she had heard about. Was it simply luck that caused them to meet that day? There is not nearly enough signage posted around downtown to assist visitors with getting around. Viewgrove cannot be described as a tourist town, at least not yet. Was it simply luck that had caused Myrtle to turn down that street? It was only her second day in town and already she was lost while trying to explore her new surroundings. The retired School Counselor had heard there was a wonderful Diner on that side of town. At one time Denise worked in an antique shop across from the massage parlor and that is where the two ladies met. Myrtle was lost and stopped into the antique shop to ask for directions. In the short time Myrtle has lived in Viewgrove they had become close friends.

"Yes, I know her, her name is Denise, Denise Washington."

CHAPTER 4

Detective Zeus pulls Myrtle to the side for a word. He can see that she is visibly upset. Standing side-by-side they look like an odd couple, the large Detective, and the little lady. At six foot four inches, Zeus towers over her five-foot frame. Although Myrtle is only five feet tall, she has the heart of a seven-foot person. Zeus knows better than to ever underestimate the little silver-haired crime solver, but this situation is different. This crime is personal to her. Had he known she was friends with the deceased he would have never brought her in on the case. Zeus feels terrible that Myrtle had to find out about her friend like this.

"I'm so sorry, I didn't know, please accept my condolences."

"I understand completely if you need to remove

yourself from the case."

Myrtle gathers her composure and a few minutes later trails Zeus back to the crime scene. "Thank you, Detective, but I have no intention of sitting this one out." The dining room is not as busy with the police officers and medical staff. The crime scene pictures have already been taken and the body is in transport to the morgue. With fewer bodies present, Myrtle is free to access the scene more easily. The guests are no longer in their seats, but the tables have not been cleared yet. The half-eaten salads remain in plain view. She examines the victim's plate and compares it to the half-eaten salad of the next guest. Myrtle has eaten a lot of salads in her day but never ones like this. They are certainly fancy, but she cannot help but wonder what is in them. So deep in thought, she has not noticed that Detective Zeus Chaplin has been standing there for the last couple of minutes. He notices the puzzling look on Myrtle's face and without being asked, explains the theme, and that the salads are supposed to resemble an English garden. Myrtle nods to acknowledge she hears him but does not take her gaze away from the salad plates. It is like those puzzles in children's activity books where they have two pictures that look the same and you must figure out what is missing from the second picture. Her eyes are not what they used to be, and she needs a closer look. In the Sherlock Holmes days, she would have pulled out her trusty magnifying glass, in these modern days, her cell phone will have to do. Ms. Jenson touches the flowers on Denise's salad. The flowers feel damp to the touch, presumably from the salad dressing. When she pulls her hand back, she notices her fingertips are stained blue. She takes a snapshot of the salad, and when enlarged it confirms her suspicion. Myrtle turns to Zeus to share her find.

Zeus gazes at the phone screen, confused at what he is supposed to be looking at. She shows him her stained fingertips that came from touching the flowers on what is left of Denise's salad. He is unimpressed, maybe all these flowers stain your fingers, he is not a botanist. The victim's salad looks the same as the other flower salads on the rest of the tables. Myrtle points to the purple hue under the fragments of cut-up flowers on Denise's plate. She asks if all the crime scene pictures have been taken, Zeus nods yes. She unrolls an unused cloth napkin from the place setting close to where Denise was sitting. Using the napkin, she picks a knife up from the table and slices into a flower on a neighboring salad and takes a picture. Once again, she zooms in and shows Zeus what is in the picture. The Detective can now see there is a difference in coloring on some of the flower petals on Denise's plate compared to the other one. He agrees that it is a little odd, but they are flowers, so he does not expect them to all be identical. The difference could be caused by a reaction to the salad dressing or something in the preparation or storage of the salad. As a compromise, he agrees to ask for a test to be run. Myrtle would have checked every salad in the room if Zeus had let her, but he needs her to process the rest of the scene. Examining a room full of salads is not the best use of their limited resources for an accident case. Detective Chaplin is following the procedure, but he starts to get a sick feeling in his stomach. If Myrtle is right about the salad being altered, what started as an unfortunate accident is now looking more like a possible murder.

Zeus turns his head toward Ms. Jenson and their eyes meet. He does not even have to say anything, the look on her face says everything he is thinking. Somethings are better left unsaid. Murders are not supposed to happen in towns like this. They both know all too well that murders happen everywhere. It hits harder for Myrtle because Denise was her friend. The day just turned from bad to worse, not only has she lost her friend today, but she now must deal with the fact it was possibly murder. Detective Zeus assures her they will get to the bottom of this, and if it turns out to be murder, they will bring whoever did this to justice. The look in Myrtle's eyes is one of determination, she thanks Zeus for his words. She believes he will do everything in his power to do what he says, and she plans to be there to help every step of the way. The Detective did not bother to ask if she wants to step away. He knows her well enough to know there is no way she is stepping down from this case now. If there is one thing he has learned from their time working together, it is that Ms. Jenson is extremely motived once she makes her mind up. Myrtle is the first to break the silence.

"I think we need to speak with the Chef."

CHAPTER 5

The duo of Myrtle and Zeus make their way into the kitchen in search of the Chef. The kitchen in this residence is huge and is fitted with professional-grade appliances. There are coolers, ovens, tray racks, and workstations. Even Zeus must acknowledge to himself that the kitchen is impressive and worthy of a home this luxurious. Myrtle likens it to something she would see in an architectural digest or decorating magazine, although she would never say that out loud. The cooks and kitchen staff are all gathered in the kitchen waiting to be released. "Has anybody seen the head Chef?", announces Detective Chaplin as they enter the room. An officer in the room points the Detective in the right direction. "Good evening Sir, my name is Detective Chaplin", he motions to his right, "This is Myrtle Jensen, a Police Consultant, may we have a few words with you?" The Chef looks them both over without uttering a word but does not nod in agreeance until Detective Chaplin flashes his Police badge. The police badge must snap the Chef out of his trance because the color returns to his face. His initial reaction to seeing the police does not go unnoticed by Myrtle, and she begins to wonder if the Chef is exhibiting signs of a guilty conscience. Zeus on the other hand is used to people being slightly unnerved when the Police approach them, his suspicions are not raised at all. He asks the Chef his name for the record.

"My name is Master Chef Tobin Crowder", he utters in a proper English accent.

Chef Crowder is a portly man which for some reason delights Myrtle. There is just something about skinny cooks that she does not trust. She is a little embarrassed to have this bias. In Myrtle's mind, food should be made with love, so how is it possible to love cooking but not love eating? When pressed she will readily admit that her theory is completely unsubstantiated by facts, and there are lots of great cooks that manage their weight well. Myrtle has no formal Chef training, she taught herself to cook by trial and error, she is out of her league compared to Chef Crowder. Detective Zeus starts with the usual opening questions about the Chef's whereabouts during the evening, especially around the time the victim choked. "Did you see or hear anything unusual tonight?" Chef Crowder insists he has been in the kitchen all day, but then he remembers he was called away a few times to handle issues with the food delivery company. He also remembers stepping outside for a cigarette by the dumpster. The Chef swears he does not know Denise or anybody who would want to harm her. Zeus makes some interview notes in his notepad. He requests a copy of the menu for the event, and the Chef motions for one of the waiters to fetch one for the Police. Myrtle is becoming more impatient with the Detective's line of questioning by the minute. She cannot contain herself any longer from addressing the elephant in the room. Turning to the Chef, she blurts out what she has been dying to know and what the Detective was working his way up to asking.

"So, you serve people flowers?"

"I beg your pardon Madam; flowers are eaten as a delicacy all over the world."

The head Chef quickly reminds Myrtle and Zeus that he is a trained professional. Chef Crowder is noticeably offended by Myrtle's line of questioning. He bites back by insinuating that Myrtle's palate is not sophisticated enough to appreciate gourmet cooking such as his. He proudly shares how, in his opinion, the best salads should be made with flowers. The head Chef educates them that what they are crudely referring to as flowers are Borage Blossoms. Borage

Blossoms are beautiful star-shaped flowers that are blue in color and have been used in salads since the Elizabethan age. They come from the borage plant and have a taste like a cucumber. The very mild cucumber tastes make them perfect for infused water and lemonades. They are also delicious in refreshing cocktails. Chef Crowder is not done, "To put it in the terms you can understand, the natural flavors of the flowers work in concert with the light vinaigrette to create a dining symphony!"

"Look, just because you're pouring syrup on it don't make it pancakes", quips Myrtle.

Detective Chaplin steps in to try to get the interview back on track. He asks the Chef to forgive them if they have offended him. Chef Crowder is a proud man and the Detective can tell he is not used to anybody criticizing his food. Zeus moves the topic away from food, and asks the Chef if he noticed anybody in the kitchen that should not have been there? Chef Crowder is more than happy to assist the Police but is becoming irritated by the number of questions. It suddenly dawns on him that Professor Weatherford and the organizers of this event could be looking to hold him responsible for what happened. He will choose his words to the Police more carefully going forward. His reputation in these high-class circles as a top Chef could be at risk so it is important not to say anything that will cause him to lose business. The Chef explains to the Detective and Myrtle that the kitchen is a very busy place during events, and it would be impossible for him to notice everybody who comes through there. Between the preparers, cooks, and waiters there are just too many people to monitor. Myrtle nudges Zeus to ask one more question about the flowers. She would ask the Chef herself, but he has stopped answering her questions since their earlier word exchange. Detective Chaplin does ask a final question of the Chef before they leave.

"Why do you paint the flowers blue?"

"What, we don't paint anything, Borage Blossoms are naturally blue."

CHAPTER 6

It is early the next morning and the Medical
Examiner, Janna, has clocked into the laboratory at
her usual time. She pours herself a generous serving
of her personal brand coffee brew into her favorite
cup that reads, 'I See Dead People' on the side. Janna
has a dark sense of humor that takes some getting
used to. Myrtle presumes Janna was one of those kids
that burned ants with magnifying glasses or enjoyed
dissecting that baby pig in biology class. Medical
Examiner is an honorable profession, and despite her
quirks, Janna is excellent at her job. Myrtle arrives
with Zeus at the Medical Examiner's office. He had
given her the option of declining this case since she
knew the victim personally. However, she would have
none of that, if anything she was more motivated to
work on the case. Before they go inside, Detective
Chaplin reminds Myrtle that her job is to consult on

murder cases. Although the circumstances of Denise's death are unusual, if the Medical Examiner rules out foul play then Myrtle is off the case. Detective Chaplin clicks the locks on the police cruiser to open, he knows she would prefer to remain in the car. Each time they work on a case he pushes Myrtle a little further out of her comfort zone. He knows she is not a fan of the morgue. Truth be told, the morgue gives her the creeps. Something about being surrounded by dead bodies makes her feel uneasy. The less time she must spend in that space the better, she would avoid it completely if she could. The only reason she even goes there is that Zeus insists on it. As a Police consultant, he wants her to become comfortable dealing with all the law enforcement departments. Having lived in town a lot longer, he also knows Viewgrove can be a town of cliques, not to mention the pockets of racism that bubble up from time to time. His goal is for all the departments to eventually become comfortable working with Myrtle.

As soon as they walk through the doors of the Medical Examiner's building Myrtle starts to feel a little nauseous. Although she identified the victim's body the day before, the Medical Examiner's Office will also contact the next of kin and use dental records for identification. They make their way into the basement where Janna is there to welcome them. Bright florescent lightboxes in the ceiling flood the room with artificial light. There is a constant low humming sound that can be heard throughout the room. The color of the walls and floor are all monotone shades of teal and gray accented by the stainless-steel gurneys and metal sinks. The room feels very cold and clinical and there is an unmistakable metallic odor in the air, possibly from a cleaning or sterilizing agent. Myrtle tries to breathe through her mouth and avoid contact with any corpses. She chooses to focus on the one flickering ceiling bulb toward the back of the room, probably in need of replacement.

"Wow, a personal visit, to what do I owe this pleasure, Detective?"

Myrtle can never quite tell if Janna is flirting with Zeus or just always this sarcastic. The only time she ever comes to the morgue is with Zeus, so she has no idea how the other men on the police force are treated. Zeus appears unfazed and always seem to take whatever she says in stride.

"You know how it is, Professor Weatherford is a friend of the Mayor", replies the Detective.

Janna gives a knowing nod as she pours herself another cup of coffee. How anybody can eat or drink anything surrounded by dead bodies is a mystery to Myrtle. The Medical Examiner raises the cup to her lips and takes a long sip before speaking again. She explains how she has ruled out choking as a cause of death. There was nothing found in Denise's airways that would have caused her to choke to death. Janna goes on to explain how the victim died from a cardiovascular event, like a heart attack. Heart attack? This makes little sense to either Myrtle or Zeus. They both are surprised to hear this. Otherwise healthy people do not normally just have heart attacks do they, how common is this? The Medical Examiner did not uncover evidence of any heart disease or previous heart attacks. It appears the waiter performed CPR correctly. Zeus asks Janna if she found anything unusual or odd in her examination of the body.

"Funny you ask, her tongue was light blue, and I found traces of flowers in her stomach."

"F-L-O-W-E-R-S in her stomach, is that a thing now?", asks Janna.

The Medical Examiner pauses and makes a face like flowers are the weirdest thing she has ever come across in a stomach. There is not so much as a chuckle from Zeus or Myrtle for her comedic efforts. She looks to Detective Zeus for validation but receives nothing, so she turns back to her coffee. Janna lets the warm coffee slide down her throat before she explains to them the blue tongue is from food coloring. Zeus discloses there were flowers in the salads that were served to the victim.

"I'm running a toxicology test; I should have the

results shortly."

True to her word, Janna returns shortly with the test results. She eyes the report while Myrtle and Zeus patiently wait with high anticipation. The pause feels a little dramatic to Myrtle, almost like she is doing it on purpose. She is reminded of one of those game shows where they go to commercial right before reading the results. Right before she is about to yell for Janna to reveal the results already, she starts talking. She explains that the death was not caused by an allergic reaction as the emergency responder's hypothesized. A reaction caused her heart to stop. Then very casually and without much inflection in her voice, Janna reveals the outcome.

"She was poisoned. The test shows traces of Foxglove, it's an extremely poisonous plant."

CHAPTER 7

Poisoned, the word keeps playing over and over in Myrtle's head as they leave the Medical Examiner's Office. If the Medical Examiner said anything after that, Myrtle did not hear it, all she could think of is that her friend was poisoned. Poisoned by something she had never even heard of before. Admittingly, poison is not a topic Myrtle has spent a lot of time researching. What is Foxglove, and how did it end up in her friend's stomach? Could it have been in the salad or did it get in her system another way? There are so many questions that need answers. Myrtle is in no mood to go straight home, she has too many thoughts to process through. She takes a drive through town to try to clear her mind. Driving through downtown is a sober reminder of how life still goes on without you. Everybody is out working or shopping, business as usual. Her drive down Main

Street takes her past the Sunset Theatre where the lit-up marquee announces the play, "The Deep Illusion" is now playing. She turns down MLK Boulevard, yes even Viewgrove has an MLK Boulevard, and makes a left on Capital Street where most of the bars and night clubs are located. Myrtle sees people walking into the bars that are open this early. She cannot help but feel tempted to pull up and join them to drown her sorrow in bottle. Myrtle is not a drinker but if ever there was a time this may be it. The desire to solve the case is greater than any desire to numb the hurt. She thinks about how it is funny that new environments can make friends of people that may not have been friends otherwise. Myrtle and Denise were not the same age, Denise was a lot younger than she is, yet they got along very well. She thought it was hilarious how Myrtle always had a saying or catch phrase for everything. She often joked with her that she should write a book of catch phrases. Their relationship reminded Myrtle of the first office she worked in out of college. She was the youngest one there, but her desk was next to Ms. Darlene. Ms. Darlene was about eight years away from retirement. Despite the age gap they developed a close bond and became particularly good friends. Whenever one was not in the office, the one would text to check in on the other. Although she was new in town, she was older, so she served as Denise's Ms. Darlene. Myrtle considered it a form of paying it forward. She would pass on bits of knowledge and advise to Denise, whether she asked for it or not. They did not talk every day, but when they did it was like they had not missed a day, how they loved to crack jokes, and laugh. Now she wishes they would have talked more. She is going to miss Denise. Life is crazy, who would have imagined Myrtle would be attending Denise's funeral and not the other way around. Speaking of the funeral, she hopes whichever family member is planning it will allow her to say a few words. It dawns on Myrtle that for all their conversations, she does not know anything about Denise's family. She makes herself a mental note to ask Zeus in the morning about Denise's next of kin. She is also curious about any funeral arrangements he may know about. She has been up since early that morning so she decides to head home to try and get some rest. Exhausted, she falls asleep for a lot longer than she had planned to.

Myrtle glances over at the alarm clock on her nightstand and sighs, it is only an hour later than when she checked it previously. It is now after one o'clock in the morning and she is still unable to fall back asleep, she just cannot turn her mind off. Viewgrove is growing but is still considered a small town. It is a fact that all cities and towns must deal with politics. Denise Washington is not a celebrity or a powerful politician in Viewgrove, however the people whose home she died in are. Myrtle knows Detective Zeus will do his best to get to the bottom of what happened no matter who is involved. She is not flatly accusing the city leaders of being corrupt, but she is not naïve. Detective Chaplin has people he reports to and they have people higher up that they report to. Pressure from the right person or office could put a lot of pressure on Detective Chaplin. She worries that the people of influence in town will demand this case be closed as soon as possible, and Denise's death will not get a thorough investigation. Unfortunately, it would not be the first time an inconvenient crime was attempted to be rushed into a closed case. Trying to sleep is not working so she gets up and goes into the living room to watch television. Myrtle lives alone so there is nobody to wake up and talk it out with. Even though he lives alone, she would not dare call Zeus at this hour. There is nothing on television at this time of night, but she is just looking for any type of distraction. Most of the programming on at this hour is infomercials, and sitcoms from twenty years ago. There is nothing like old reruns to put you to sleep. The television stays on while she lays on the couch staring at the ceiling. She is thankful for the white noise, and eventually nods off to sleep from pure exhaustion. Myrtle's sleep is not a peaceful one, she tosses and turns from a nightmare she will not remember in the morning. The tossing and turning prevent her from falling into a deep sleep and cause her to wake up briefly a few more times throughout the night.

CHAPTER 8

The sunrise shines through the living room blinds announcing it is morning. Myrtle has not used an alarm clock to wake up since she retired, but her body is programmed to still wake up early. She is disappointed in herself for spending the whole night on the couch. To make matters worse, she got absolutely no sleep. After a hot shower, she is dressed and en route to her first stop. That first stop is the drive-thru of a fast-food restaurant for a cup of coffee, a sausage and cheese breakfast sandwich, all with the senior discount. She drags herself back to the Police station bright and early to go over the case evidence. Zeus is surprised to see her in so early, he wishes she would take a few days off to grieve. She looks like she has been up all night, but he will keep that comment to himself. He knows trying to send her home will be a waste of time. Part of being a good detective is knowing your audience. Contrary to his superiors, Detective Zeus Chaplin believes Denise Washington was murdered by poison. Janna, the medical examiner, is quirky but she knows her stuff. Furthermore, he is convinced Myrtle was the intended target. The fact that she was supposed to be at that dinner event is not lost on Myrtle. Based on the evidence currently available, it is a reasonable theory. Besides, who would want to harm Denise?

"Zeus, I know it's early, but do we have any updates on the case?"

"Nothing yet, but I have advised everyone not to leave town, including the Chef."

Myrtle expects Detective Zeus to request everybody to remain in town, but it is still nice to hear him say it. Speaking of being in town, who would know she was going to be attending the dinner? She decides to take another look at the guest list. They both glanced over the guest list yesterday but being in shock she could have easily missed a name or two. There is always a possibility of a name triggering a memory the second time around. It is hard for her to believe she would have any enemies, but who can ever be sure. Zeus is called away to a conference call with the Chief, leaving her to work on the case alone.

Myrtle combs over the guest list thoroughly, line by line, and name by name in hopes to discover something or someone out of place. Most of the guest list is comprised of high-profile people around town, it is a virtual who's who of Viewgrove. Some of the guests are from the business industry and own some of the largest companies in town with their names splashed across their storefronts. Other names have appeared in the entertainment section of the Viewgrove Gazette at one time or another. Myrtle is not up to date on the latest pop culture news, but she still recognizes some of the celebrity names while not knowing what they are famous for. Is Samantha Starwood that singer WVG12 featured on their 10 o'clock newscast, the one that came in tenth on that televised singing competition? Perhaps that was Birdie Irish, and she was confusing the two, either way, Myrtle had heard of the names on the list somewhere. Viewgrove is not Hollywood but they still have local celebrities and socialites. The list included out of town guests, having just arrived for the occasion, she assumes they are important people wherever they are from. The guest list also includes some local elected officials.

Zeus's theory is that the poison was payback for a previous case Myrtle had worked on. He feels the best approach is to pour over all the old cases that she has worked to see if anybody would have a reason to want her dead. Myrtle logs into the file archives and realizes she has worked on more cases than she thought. Only two of the cases fit the criteria, looks like this may not provide the clues they are hoping for. Ever since she agreed to become a Police Consultant, Zeus has been trying to stress the importance of working with different departments and within the team. She does not want to openly dismiss his theory about the old cases, but she would rather focus on who knew she was going to be at the event. If she runs into a dead end, perhaps she will then consider following up on those old cases, but not a moment before that. With town officials present it is possible the target was someone in local government. The motive could be the same. Perhaps it is in retaliation for a bill they worked on? With all these local dignitaries and local celebrities in attendance, it dawns on her that the poison could have been meant for anybody on that guest list. Zeus had just assumed it was meant for her, but there were lots of local celebrities present. Who knows what enemies these guests have accumulated on their way to fame and fortune? The salad plates could have gotten mixed up with the poisoned one ending up in front of Denise, instead of the intended target. Zeus feels even more confident about his theory since all the interviewed guests claim they do not have any enemies.

CHAPTER 9

The suspect board that Detective Chaplin has constructed has a lot of gaps in it. It currently consists of names from Myrtle's old file cases that he has yet to comb through. A few of the ones that stick out to her are Martin Goodwill, aka 'Goody', Ms. Claudine Washington, and Wendy Gates, aka 'Ms. Marmalade'. There were some important people at the banquet, important people who may like this case closed quickly. Denise was by no means considered high society in Viewgrove, so it is not a stretch to say some of them would not be opposed to ruling it an accident. Myrtle would like to be able to trace the last hours of her friend's life. Denise's phone is one of the personal effects wrapped in plastic evidence bags. The cell phone was in her clutch purse, but the phone screen is locked. Myrtle would love to see any pictures Denise took that night. Maybe her killer is in one of them? Perhaps she captured something that would be useful in figuring out a motive?

Unfortunately, the Police are unable to unlock her phone. The Police have reached out to the cell phone manufacturer, but they refuse to unlock the phone. Myrtle is not surprised; cell phone producers are known to deny these kinds of requests even in high profile cases. None of the Viewgrove Police Brass are willing to escalate the unlock request to the higher ups at the manufacturer because they do not feel it is essential to closing the case. Had it have been one of those phones equipped with fingerprint ID or face recognition they may have been successful, although the process would be a little morbid. Myrtle selfishly had hoped to see a few more pictures of her friend. She examines the rest of the contents from Denise's purse, they have all been bagged and tagged and now lay spread out across the desk. There is a tube of lipstick, a compact, hand sanitizer, a cell phone, some keys, a driver's license, and a small wallet with a few credit cards and cash. This is not her main purse because there are not that many items in there, just the essentials a person takes when they are going out on a date or to an event. Myrtle's everyday handbag is always packed with a few pounds of stuff she might need.

A phone ringing on a neighboring desk interrupts this police consultant's train of thought. That reminds her, she needs to place a call to the catering company. Chef Crowder does not travel with a full waitstaff. The staff that worked the event were supplied by Let's Eat Catering Company. On the night of the murder, Myrtle had asked the manager if anybody called in sick that day, and if any equipment was missing? The catering manager, Joe, could not answer the questions back then but can answer today. After going through the inventory everything appears to be accounted for, minus a missing basting brush, a spoon, a broken glass, and two broken saucers. According to Joe, it is not unusual for a few items to be missing or broken after a big event. Then he remembers, there is a red waiter's jacket missing, the staff is usually incredibly good at keeping up with their uniform. Joe is careful to say it may be just misplaced. Seven waiters, including the waiter who is assigned the jacket, did not show up for work today. According to Joe, it is a common occurrence after big events where the clients tip the working staff directly. It is the main reason they ask clients not to tip the working staff. "You must lose tons of waiter jackets there don't you?" asks Myrtle. "The opposite", explains Joe, "The waiters are independent contractors that work for us part-time, we cannot afford to keep that large a staff on our regular payroll. Clients pay a lot of money, so the jackets are tailored to custom fit each waiter, the staff must look good. The waiters take exceptional care of their uniforms because if your jacket doesn't fit, you can't work." He promises to call her if the missing jacket turns up.

So far Myrtle does not have much to go on, she hopes the pictures will be more helpful. Perhaps there is a picture of somebody that is out of place or if she is lucky, a picture of a waiter serving the salad. Fortunately, a professional photographer and videographer were hired to cover the event. Perfect Vision has been operating in Viewgrove for over 20 years. Everybody in town is familiar with their slogan, "Perfect Vision, for pictures worth more than a thousand words." Their services are known to be pricy, but they do quality work and are well respected around town. The photographer Perfect Vision assigned took a lot of pictures and video, including a lot of candid shots that would never make it to a professional print release. The photographer turned the whole digital camera roll over to the Police as evidence. Myrtle takes a long sip of the large coffee she got from the drive-thru on her way to the Police station. She is not a fan of the specialty coffee; she prefers her coffee with sweetener and half-n-half creamer. A valuable clue could be hidden in these photos and videos, and she needs to be alert enough to catch it.

Myrtle is admittedly not very technically savvy when it comes to a computer but fortunately, there is an officer there to set it up for her. She is always amazed by what can be done with technology these days. The paid photographer did a great job of capturing every table at different points of the evening, there are a lot of pictures to go through in the gallery. She takes her time combing through pictures of table setting, pictures of guests, and even pictures of salads with flowers. Ironically, blue was Denise's favorite color. To her disappointment, none of the faces match anybody she remembers helping to convict on any of her old cases. Unfortunately, none of the pictures show who served Denise the salad. Even if there was it would be hard to tell because the waiters are all wearing black carnival-style eye masks, it must be a party theme. Myrtle is a little surprised that nothing in the pictures initially jumps out to her as being out of place.

The pictures supplied by Perfect Vision do turn out to be especially useful for identifying the guests though. She will need to speak with some of the guests in the pictures, starting with the lady who was sitting right next to Denise when she died. Perhaps this lady saw something that the photographer's camera missed. It is time to visit Mrs. Fannie Dubai. Her eyelids start to feel heavy from the combination of looking at all those pictures on the computer monitor and lack of sleep. Some fresh air would do her body a world of good. She yawns as she grabs her purse and heads for the door. On her way out she thanks the young officer for his help. Detective Zeus Chaplin returns from his meeting looking for Myrtle so they can comb over some of her old cases and determine who would want to kill her.

"Has anybody seen Ms. Jenson?"

"She left about ten minutes ago Detective."

Zeus thinks it is a odd that she left without saying anything but he knows this case is going to affect her different than that the others did. He will give her time to recharge herself. He also knows Myrtle likes to act on her hunches, but as long as nobody is calling him to come pick her up he is fine. He pulls up some of the old case files and starts to look over them for a possible connection.

CHAPTER 10

The theory of six degrees of separation is the idea that all people are six or fewer social connections away from each other. At this moment Myrtle cannot think of anybody close enough to Fannie Dubai to provide an introduction. She has always heard that Mrs. Dubai and others like her were members of the exclusive Margallo Tennis Club, so she decides to head over there and casually bump into her. The Margallo Tennis Club is more of a social club for the upper crust of Viewgrove, few members even play tennis. This is Myrtle's first trip to the Club, and it is just as she pictured it would be. The property is complete with well-manicured lawns and foreign luxury cars in the parking lot. Myrtle's plan is immediately halted when the clerk at the front desk will not admit her without a membership. The desk clerk punctuates her response with an open gesture toward the exit.

"I'm interested in joining and would like a quick tour", suggests Myrtle.

"One cannot just join the Margallo, you must be referred by a member", comes the snooty reply.

On the way to her car, she notices a bread delivery truck drive past and disappears around the corner. It is going to take more than a snarky desk clerk to derail the mission. Myrtle stealthily makes her way around the same path as the truck to the service entrance in the back of the property. The workers are too busy to pay her any attention as she walks into the building. Myrtle makes her way from the loading dock and through the kitchen. The kitchen smells like fresh-baked bread, it smells wonderful. She lifts an apron hanging from a nearby wall hook and grabs a serving tray from a stack waiting to be washed. Using the serving tray to hide her face, she slips into the main dining room for a look around. The lunch rush must be over because the dining room is almost empty. On one of the vacated tables, the guests have left their basket of honey wheat brown bread untouched, which is criminal. That must be what they are baking in the kitchen, she loves those honey wheat brown bread mini loaves with the rolled oats sprinkled on top, and wonders if they sell them there. Myrtle refocuses, there is no sign of Mrs. Dubai or anybody else from the pictures. A young server sits in the corner of the room folding cutlery into cloth napkins for place settings. She is startled by the old black lady who has suddenly appeared in front of her asking questions.

"Everybody knows tomorrow is Mrs. Dubai's normal day. Are you new?"

"Yes, I'm a temp, today's my first day", lies Myrtle.

With the young server still eyeing her suspiciously, Myrtle retreats through the kitchen, tossing the apron in the laundry cart on the way out of the building. She can hear somebody yelling, "Hey, that doesn't go there!", but she dares not stop or look back.

Mrs. Fannie Dubai lives in a huge house in the hills. Myrtle pulls up to her security gate and pushes the buzzer on the speaker box. "Yes, can we help you", crackles a voice through the speaker. "Myrtle Jensen to see Ms. Fannie Dubai", she responds to the voice on the other end. There is a short pause and then a buzzer sound as the iron gate parts and allows access to the long driveway. She throws her car into gear and proceeds up to the top of the circular driveway. It is unclear where to park so she parks just short of what looks like the front door. Myrtle looks around before she gets out of her car, just in case guard dogs are waiting to greet her as soon as she steps out. She does not mind dogs; she just hates them jumping on her, and worse, vicious dogs that bite. In her opinion, you have got to watch all dogs regardless of what their owners say. "Oh, he doesn't bite", they would say, to which she always responds, "he has teeth doesn't he." The driveway is all clear, so she takes one last look before getting out. The doorbell sounds like church bells ringing. The sun is up, and it is another beautiful day in Viewgrove. Myrtle has dressed appropriately for the weather in one of her new skirts. She does not wear pants, so she is always on the lookout for new skirts. The door swings open and she is greeted by whom she assumes is the butler. Upon entering the grand foyer, guests are greeted by a huge cylindrical salt-water aquarium filled with live coral and tropical fish. Myrtle cannot help but admire the aquarium, "This is so beautiful, look at all of these colorful fish, what kind of fish is that one?" The butler stops to look, "That there is a Pterois, commonly known as a lionfish. It is a venomous coral reef fish and one of the madam's favorites." He then proceeds to lead her into a nearby parlor. In the middle of the parlor is a beautiful bouquet of fresh exotic-looking flowers displayed on a round mahogany table. Her eyes pan over the well-furnished room before abruptly meeting the gaze of a stone-faced Mrs. Fannie Dubai.

Myrtle introduces herself and apologizes for the inconvenience of showing up uninvited. "Yes!" bellows Mrs. Dubai with a wide grin, "Myrtle Jenson, we finally meet, may I call you MJ?" Myrtle shakes her head, "Ms. Jenson is just fine." Her face gives away what she is thinking. "Oh, don't look like that, I like to know whom I'm sitting next to at these events." She is now more curious than ever about what else her host knows. Since she appears to know who she is, they can skip the formal introductions. If Zeus were there, he would have provided full introductions. Mrs. Dubai offers Myrtle a cup of coffee and she accepts. "Cream and sugar Ms. Jenson?" Myrtle asks if she may have half and half and sweetener instead. Minutes later the same manservant that answered the door arrives with a tray of coffee and the prettiest coffee set she has ever seen. On the tray were also several types of cookies, Myrtle is always looking for a good cookie, "Don't mind if I do." Mrs. Dubai sits across the table and helps herself to one of the butter cookies. Myrtle is struck by the number of rings on her host's fingers as she reaches out for a cookie, every finger had a ring on it. "This lady does dress like this every day", she thought to herself. Mrs. Dubai is just as dressed up now as she was the day of the dinner. She knows from the pictures that Fannie was seated closest to Denise that night, so she asks if she saw or heard anything unusual? Fannie Dubai is happy to share what she saw, "Well, the dinner had just started, and I was enjoying my salad when I heard the ghastliest sound coming from beside me." She describes how it all happened so quickly, one minute the young lady was enjoying her salad, and the next she was on the floor. The emcee rushed to the microphone and announced for everybody to remain calm and that the police and paramedics were on their way. She assures Ms. Jenson that Denise was fine before that and displayed no signs of sickness. Mrs. Dubai did not know Denise but claims she cannot imagine anybody wanting to hurt her. She expresses her condolences and how it was a shame Denise had an allergic reaction. "Would you mind showing me your hands?", asks Ms. Jenson. "Well, aren't you an odd one", laughs Mrs. Dubai, while standing up to signal their visit was over but not showing her hands. Ms. Jenson wonders how this lady knew Denise did not choke, the Police have not even released Denise's name to the public, let alone her cause of death.

"So, the Police suspect foul play?"

"The Police haven't concluded anything", replies Ms. Jenson.

To Myrtle's surprise, Fannie Dubai is a gossip. There is a Mr. Dubai but rumor has it he is always away on business. It could partly explain why Fannie spends so much time staying up to date on all the town gossip. Mrs. Dubai has a lot of major business contracts around town, and in the big business circles, it is not a secret how much she loves to gossip. The result is a lot of people throw in local gossip and dirt on their competitors to gain favor with her in their business dealings. It works out well for Mrs. Dubai because she gets her gossip fix, but she also gets to use the inside information to leverage deals in her favor in her contract negotiations. One of these connections must have tipped her off on the Police investigation. Denise is somebody she did not know much about, but she is just dying to find out all the juicy details. Myrtle thanks her gracious host for seeing her and makes her way back to her car. Glancing back, she can make out Mrs. Dubai's silhouette in the picture window watching her. One thing is clear, Fannie Dubai knew Myrtle would be at the award dinner, and where she would be sitting. The big question is why would she want to kill her?

CHAPTER 11

On Myrtle's drive back into town her cell phone rings, it is Detective Chaplin. Zeus tells her Chef Crowder contacted him because he has remembered something that may be important to the case. The Chef was not very forthcoming the first time they spoke to him but since then he has been restricted from leaving town. Zeus believes the Chef has had a change of heart because he wants to get out of Viewgrove. He doubts the Chef could have no more than two cooking events in town, his real money is made elsewhere. He tells Myrtle he is on his way to meet with the Chef now, and she is welcome to join him if she is free. Oh, she is free, she will make time for this. Myrtle Jenson is very curious about what the Chef has to say. Once she pulls up the address from her GPS history, the calm navigation voice immediately tells her she is going the wrong way, recalculating. She will make it a point to take a hard look at the Chef for any signs they have crossed paths before. Chef Crowder is a person of interest if for no other reason than he was the chef that night. Zeus has instructed her to wait for him before approaching the Chef. The last time Myrtle spoke with the Chef it did not go so well. She does not have to wait in the parking lot long before Zeus's police issued sedan pulls up. The vehicle is not black and white with badging, but it still screams police car. It is a relief to find Myrtle waiting for him, a small part of him half expected to find her trying to interview the Chef without him.

"It's about time you got here," sasses Myrtle.

"Interesting you beat me here, I drove the speed limit, how about you?" he teases back.

Detective Chaplin explains they are at Chef Crowder's next engagement. This is probably the last one he has in town. The engagement is a private event by invitation only. One of the wealthy guests is a big supporter of the police fundraiser benefit and provided the Police with a copy of their invitation to the second event. Without that tip the police department may have had a harder time locating Chef Crowder. Zeus knows once this event concludes the Chef is free to leave Viewgrove. Simply being the Chef makes him a person of interest. He hopes this interview either clears Chef Crowder or gives them a reason to investigate him further.

Zeus is first through the kitchen double swing doors with Myrtle close behind him. The kitchen is spotless, it does not look like there is a speckle of food or splashed sauce on any of the surfaces. Whenever Myrtle cooks the kitchen ends up looking a total mess. The Chef is busy talking to a line cook but looks up and acknowledges the Detective by waiving him over. The color falls out of Chef Crowder's face when he sees Myrtle stroll into the kitchen behind Zeus. "Who let you into my kitchen?", barks Chef Crowder. Myrtle cannot help but notice the big stainless-steel bowl of cut flowers chilling in an ice bath on the counter behind the Chef.

"Tell me you're not still cooking with flowers, unbelievable!"

"I've told you, flowers are my specialty, it's part of the reason people hire me."

Chef Crowder points toward the two big blackboards to the right of him with the night's menu written out in chalk. On the menu, for an appetizer is the blossom botanical garden salad he was just bragging about. For the main course, a choice of either Camarata Nero served with Dungeness crab, tomato, chili, and gremolata or Wagyu Striploin served with marrow butter, gremolata, demi-glace. The sides are either Grilled Chicories with watermelon radish and anchovy vinaigrette or Fingerling Potatoes with salsa verde and sea salt. For dessert, a choice of either Cranberry Sherbet in Tuile cups or Baked Chocolate Mousse with cream and raspberries. "Whatever happened to regular food?", mumbles Myrtle under her breath to the Detective but still loud enough for the Chef to hear. Just to instigate she suggests the Chef's guests may appreciate other choices of sides, like spaghetti, coleslaw, and even French fries. Zeus hates when she does this and shoots her a disapproving look. Chef Crowder is visibly shaken and is turning a bright shade of red, "Spaghetti is not a side dish. I suppose you put ketchup on everything and carry hot sauce in your purse too!" That last comment hits close to home because truth be told she does carry hot sauce in her purse. Nevertheless, she will not give him the satisfaction of being correct, so she plays every bit of being offended. "Would you mind showing us your hands?", asks Myrtle. Chef Crowder outstretches his hands to reveal he is wearing a pair of black latex gloves.

Detective Chaplin needs every bit of his de-escalation training to regain control of the conversation. Chef Crowder calms down, "Where are my manners, it's teatime, can I offer you some tea and cake?" To Myrtle's surprise, Zeus takes the Chef up on his offer. A teapot with cups and cakes is quickly set up on the counter. The cake looks delicious but there is no way she is taking anything from Chef

Crowder, just on principle. After a few sips of tea, the Chef reveals that he remembers one of the waiters was missing at the end of that night of the event. Zeus was confused as to how he would even notice since the waiters came from the Let's Eat Catering Company. The Chef explains that whenever he goes on location, he interviews all the waitstaff the catering company sends over and picks the ones he likes the best. The guests that attend his events are not expected to tip the waitstaff. At the end of each night, he has made it customary to give each worker a bonus for a job well done. Despite their protests, Chef Crowder does not trust the catering company to distribute the bonus money to the workers. Even on the night of the death, tragic as it was, the Chef did not want to break tradition by not paying everybody their bonus. "Did you see or hear anything unusual that night?", asks Zeus. The Chef takes a minute before answering, yes, he had one bonus check leftover that night. He motions for the Detective and Myrtle to follow him into a back office. It appears to be his base of operations while he is in town. They both notice the Chef pull out a key, he must keep the office locked. The office is modestly furnished with a few chairs, a desk, filing cabinets, and a safe. Myrtle walks over to the window, and while the Chef is distracted, she unlocks the latch. Chef Crowder rumbles through a briefcase set in a desk drawer and produces a white envelope with something written on it. The envelope contains the waiter's bonus money.

"I have an event to plan for, I trust you can get this money to him."

Detective Chaplin accepts the envelope with a promise to get it to the waiter. Myrtle feels the Chef should deliver his own mail and is shocked he took the envelope. Zeus thanks the Chef for his time and ushers himself and Myrtle out the door. She would have loved to stay and poke around that kitchen, but Zeus gently reminds her they do not have a warrant. Even after seeing him again, she does not remember ever crossing paths with Chef Crowder, but he could have lost a lot of weight or cut his hair. She feels like she would have for sure remembered the English accent. Could he somehow be connected to one of her previous cases? It turns out the Detective was playing a little good cop to Myrtle's bad cop to gain a little cooperation from Chef Crowder. Zeus and Myrtle huddle around the trunk of his car, he still has the envelope in his hand and Myrtle is dying to see the name on it. He flips it over so they can both read the name, 'Jean Pierre'.

CHAPTER 12

Zeus must get back to the police station, so Myrtle makes plans to meet up with him later. Before parting ways, the Detective asks her if she recognizes the name on the envelope. Myrtle thinks hard but draws a blank. There is always a chance this waiter is using an alias. Now that they have a name, Zeus feels confident he will be able to track down the waiter for an interview. There was initially hope, at least in her mind, that the Chef interview would provide Zeus with enough information to charge somebody and make an arrest. Unfortunately, that is not what happened. The Detective pulled her out of the kitchen interview, but she is convinced the Chef may be hiding something, if only she could ask a few more questions. So far, they have not been able to link any of these people to Myrtle's old cases. It is no accident that the Chef gave them that envelope. She wonders if he is helping or trying to divert the attention from himself. Right then she makes her mind up, she must see what else is in that back office. If there is nothing there, then she will cross the Chef off her list of suspects. Myrtle needs a way back into the kitchen office without being detected. Walking through the main door without Detective Chaplin will just get her escorted out or possibly arrested for trespassing. The first thing she does is drive her vehicle away from the front parking lot to appear as though she has left. Professor Weatherford rents out the manor several times per year. On the top floor on the manor is a remolded residence. The Professor maintains a separate grand residence in another part of town. The residence in the manor is usually rented out to the clients that rent the manor. Professor Weatherford makes a sizeable amount of income from the rentals. The grand ballroom and professional kitchen make the manor a desirable venue. Myrtle pulls her car around to the parking lot marked staff. Her shiny black luxury sedan sticks out among the older model vehicles parked in the lot. She tries to hide it by parking behind a late 90's conversion van. If the staff parking lot is under security camera surveillance, hopefully they will not notice her car there.

Myrtle changes into the tennis shoes she keeps in the trunk for her senior cardio class at the YMCA. Sneaking around the grounds of the manor would be a little easier if it were dark outside. A black hat and a pair of sunglasses complete her makeshift disguise, there is no time to come up with something better. If this were a Mission Impossible movie, she would be wearing a latex face mask that she could rip off from the neck once the mission was complete. The Mission Impossible theme music plays in her head as she makes her way toward the Weatherford manor. The story she heard was Professor Weatherford's family is very wealthy, so he teaches for the status of it and not to earn a living. This explains how he can afford to own and restore such an extravagant property. Myrtle Jenson sneaks around the perimeter of the building, peering into windows while at the same time trying to avoid security cameras. Unsure how close she is, she keeps going, one of these windows must be the kitchen office. Just as she is about to abort the mission, she sees a familiar sight up ahead. It is a Zen garden; the same one she saw from inside the office earlier. Unlocking the window is a trick she saw on some tv show years ago, who knew it had a chance of working in real life. In the distance behind her, she can hear a leaf blower getting closer and louder, she needs to squeeze herself through this window immediately. Peering into the office window she can see somebody, presumably Chef Crowder, seated at the desk. Myrtle is caught between the Chef in the office and the approaching groundskeeper. The roar of the leaf blower is getting louder and louder, surely this groundskeeper will come around the corner any minute and discover her there. Chef Crowder finishes whatever he was working on and turns the light off as he leaves the room. The lock clicks as he closes the door behind him. The minute he leaves, she rips off the screen cover, pushes up the windowpane, and throws her body through it headfirst. It sounds as if the leaf blower is right behind her as her legs clear the windowsill.

Myrtle tries her best to muffle the thud made by her body hitting the floor inside the office. Climbing through windows is not easy, those windows are higher off the floor than she thought. She pauses for a few minutes to catch her breath. Regret creeps in, maybe she should not have done this, but it is too late now, she is inside. Myrtle removes her sunglasses and tries to let her eyes adjust to the darkness. She does not dare to risk turning the office light back on for fear of being discovered. With no flashlight on hand, the light from the flashlight mode on her cell phone will have to do. It is a short distance to the desk. Myrtle is not moving as quickly as she usually does, the jump through the window took a lot out of her. The phone light rolls over the desk searching for anything of interest. The light reveals a desk calendar, a phone, but nothing personal. There is no way to know how long before the Chef returns to the office. She tries the desk drawers and finds the one with the briefcase in it. To her surprise, the briefcase has no lock on it. Inside the briefcase are documents, receipts, contracts, and other things that appear to be related to the Chef's business. Earlier research did reveal the Chef owns a few restaurants. Chef Crowder is surprisingly organized. In the briefcase, there is a folder marked Viewgrove. In the folder is the contact information for Let's Eat Catering Company, the address to the manor, along with hotel and car rental information. There are notes about produce and meats which she assumes to be related to the event menus. So far, the only thing the Chef is hiding are room dimensions, estimates, ledgers, and price quotes. The last thing at the bottom of the briefcase is an unsigned contract offer to Chef Crowder Inc. from a company named Lionfish LLC. Skimming the contract, it appears the Chef would be selling a controlling interest in his company holdings to Lionfish LLC. With no regard for the poor lighting, she snaps pictures of the contract before carefully returning it to where she found it. Somebody can be heard having a conversation right outside of the door. Myrtle quickly makes her way back to the window and heaves herself out. The lock clicks just as she is replacing the window screen. In walks Chef Crowder, he stops and looks around the room like he senses somebody has been in there. He walks over toward the window, unaware of the person below desperate to stay out of view. Her heart is racing, and her knees are burning from squatting up tightly against the building. Just then the sprinkler system turns on, soaking the plant beds. The Chef figures it must be the sprinklers he heard and walks back to his desk.

After giving it a few minutes to ensure the coast is clear, a sore and soaked Myrtle scurries back to her car. She does not get twenty steps before she is spotted and stopped by security. The security officer does not consider a limping soaking wet senior as much of a security threat, so he simply walks her to the parking lot and warns her not to return. Myrtle could not care less who saw her now, all she can think about is going home and getting out of those wet clothes.

CHAPTER 13

Zeus Chaplin contacts the Let's Eat Catering
Company to try to obtain an address for the waiter
Jean Pierre. The Detective swings by to pick up
Myrtle from her home, he knows he would have to
listen to fussing for days if he interviewed the waiter
without her. Myrtle gingerly lowers herself into the
passenger seat. She knows he notices her stiff
movement and wonders when he will bring it up.
Zeus instead decides to comment on the fact she
came to the car with a different wardrobe than when
he just saw her earlier. "Is this your interview outfit?",
he asks. "I got soaked, it's a long story Detective, I
don't even want to get into it right now." Zeus is not
okay with illegally entering a building and she knows
it. She is quite sure he can smell the pain relief
ointment she rubbed on to soothe her joints, but he is
too much of a gentleman to mention it. A few

minutes later he and Myrtle are on their way to visit
Mr. Pierre. They pull up to a block of apartment
buildings that look more like motels with the exterior
walk-up staircases. According to Zeus, this area is
known for leasing units and rooms month-to-month.
The Detective asks Myrtle to wait by the car while he
speaks to the leasing manager. The leasing manager
wants the police out of his hair as soon as possible, so
he gives up the spare room key without any protest.
Zeus makes his way up the stairway while waiving to
Myrtle to come on up. She is exiting the police cruiser
at the same time Jean Pierre is exiting his apartment
unit with a suitcase. Jean Pierre is headed right toward
Zeus until he catches sight of the Detective coming
up the stairs. Immediately he takes off running in the
opposite direction on the catwalk toward the stairway
on the opposite end. Zeus takes off up the stairs after
him, while yelling police and ordering him to stop. He
shows no signs of stopping, even after colliding with
an unsuspecting neighbor and causing their laundry
basket full of clothes to scatter all over the catwalk.
Jean Pierre has a large enough head start that he is still
able to make it to the opposite stairway before Zeus
can catch up to him. A few steps to go before he is in
the parking lot and then to his car. His foot clears the
bottom step on the stairway and just as he is about to
hit the parking lot, bang, something hits him from the
side. Jean Pierre rolls around on the parking lot
pavement for a minute trying to catch his breath. He
had been so focused on Zeus that he had not noticed

Myrtle pushing a big recycling bin into him as he exited the stairway. As he tried to get up, he heard a voice ordering him to stay down, and this time he listened.

Zeus leans over Jean Pierre and flashes his badge before formally introducing himself. "My name is Detective Chaplin, this is Myrtle Jenson, do you have a minute to answer a few questions?" Jean Pierre is still trying to figure out what happened. He is out of breath, his luggage is scattered across the parking lot, and he is lying in garbage. The best he can do is manage a half nod. Zeus gives Myrtle a thumbs up for her quick thinking. He then helps to lift Jean off the parking lot ground and marches him back up to his apartment. It was either talk to them in his apartment or down at the police station, and the waiter chose his apartment. The truth is if it were not for her being so sore, she would have been right behind Zeus on the stairs. The reason she was still downstairs is she was looking for an elevator. Myrtle gathers the waiter's luggage and lumbers slowly up the stairs to apartment 205. She feels the judgment as she walks past the small crowd of spectators that has gathered to see what all the noise is about. Surprisingly, the apartment door is locked, forcing her to knock. Zeus peeks out the window before letting her in. "Can't be too careful", he explains, "He may have sympathetic neighbors." Jean Pierre is sitting at an old kitchen table with a cup of tap water. The apartment has worn beige carpeting and smells like the last tenant had pets or smoked, maybe both. Myrtle is relieved to be able to put Jean's luggage down, it was getting heavy. Zeus looks at the bag and then at Jean Pierre.

"Are you going somewhere, Mr. Pierre?"

"Yes, I'm going on a short vacation."

The look on Zeus's face clearly says he is not buying that. Jean Pierre begins nervously babbling on about taking a short vacation he had planned last minute and working long hours. Meanwhile, Myrtle looks around the bathroom and through the bedroom. It does not give the appearance that he ever planned on returning, there is not a single personal item left behind. She checks every closet in the apartment and there is no sign of the waiter's jacket. "Where is your waiter's jacket Mr. Pierre?", she asks, "Is it in the bag you packed?" Jean Pierre swears he does not know where the jacket is and dares her to check his bag. Myrtle looks to Zeus for his reaction. "Sounds like consent to me!" The bag has a lock on it. She looks at Jean Pierre whose eyes reflexively glance at the ring of keys on the table before looking away. It was too late; he has betrayed himself and the look on his face says he knows it. Myrtle lifts Jean Pierre's ring of keys off the table and tries each key until she finds the one that unlocks the bag. She is sure she will find the missing waiter jacket but after going through the contents she finds nothing. There is everything you need to leave town in a hurry but there is no waiter's jacket. Jean Pierre leans back into his chair with a 'told you so' expression on his face.

Detective Zeus Chaplin doubles down and explains how it looks for where he is sitting. "Mr. Pierre, you don't show up for work, we find you with a packed bag, and you try to run from us." Jean Pierre continues to insist he has done nothing wrong; they appear to be going in circles. "Why did you run?" inquires Myrtle. "I thought you were sent", replies Jean Pierre as if he is lost in thought, almost in a trance. Myrtle is confused, "You thought who sent us?" Jean comes back to himself and refuses to say more. Myrtle tries a different approach and asks a professional question. "I'm curious, at a Chef Crowder event, how do the waiters know who gets which meal?" Mr. Pierre is not sure if his interviewers are playing a game of good cop bad cop, but the question seems harmless enough. He explains to her how Chef Crowder has a specific numbering system he uses for each table. The salads are prepared earlier in the day, set on serving trays, and placed in the cooler until serving time. He serves very high-end clients, so he is extremely particular about his system. The serving trays are custom, they have numbers embossed on them that correspond to the seats at the table. That way he can make sure guests with dietary needs are accommodated. "Rumor has it he lost a major account and had to rebuild his reputation after a waiter mistakenly served a guest the wrong meal." Zeus let Mr. Pierre finish his story before asking him if he saw or heard anything unusual that night? Jean Pierre casually states he cannot recall seeing anything unusual that night. The response is too casual for the Detective's liking. He decides to disclose that Denise was possibly poisoned by something in the salad that night.

"Where were you at the time of Denise Washington's death?"

The waiter starts to put two and two together. "No, no, wait a minute, anybody could have put that flower in the salad." He protests that it is not like flowers are on the banned substances list, in fact, any greenhouse sells all kinds of flowers. He suggests somebody at the greenhouse may have mixed up an order and the wrong flower got mixed into the Chef's batch. "Probably some teenage employee that was not paying attention." Zeus asks Mr. Pierre if he was at the manor the whole night. Jean Pierre sighs and plants his face in both hands. As he did so Myrtle makes sure to get a good look at his hands, but she can only see the back-hand side. "I worked that night, but I left early because I didn't feel well, that's all I know." Zeus has nothing to charge Jean Pierre with, so he gives him a stern warning not to leave town. The two of them leave the waiter in the apartment and head back to the car.

"I don't think he's connected to any of my old cases but he's hiding something", mutters Myrtle.

"Most people are, doesn't mean he's our killer", responds the Detective, "Oh shoot, I forgot to give him the envelope."

CHAPTER 14

The interview with the waiter did not reveal a whole lot, but during his protest, he did say something about a greenhouse. He could have said nursery or some other generic term, in Myrtle's mind, Jean Pierre may have unwillingly dropped a clue. A google search reveals two greenhouses in the area. Myrtle studies the results, "The first search result is the closest, a company named the Greenhouse Garden Center." Zeus turns on the flashing patrol lights, the tires screech as he executes an illegal U-turn in the middle of the street, "Hold on, I know where that is." Myrtle did not even have to talk him into visiting the Greenhouse Garden Center, he already knew what she was thinking. He knows she is very motivated to find the killer, but he also knows the trail on some of these cases can grow cold quickly. If this trip to the Greenhouse does not produce any suspects there is little left to go on. He wonders if she is prepared for that possibility. Zeus gently approaches the subject and suggests that after they leave the Greenhouse Garden Center, they could both pay a visit to whoever was sitting next to Denise at the dinner event. He admits it is a long shot, but they may have some information that could be useful. There was Mrs. Dubai on the one side but the other side appeared empty. Whoever was supposed to be there apparently failed to show up. Myrtle feels compelled to confess that she has already visited Mrs. Dubai. She can tell by the look on his face that he is not so happy to learn this. Mrs. Dubai has enough influence in Viewgrove to cause a lot of problems for the Detective and the Viewgrove Police Department. "Please tell me you didn't do anything illegal to secure that meeting, wait, on second thought don't tell me."

Zeus takes a shortcut, so they arrive at their destination in no time at all, the Mrs. Dubai conversation will have to wait. The Greenhouse Garden Center is a surprisingly modern operation, there is a main indoor building surrounded by various gardens and nurseries. The initial picture in Myrtle's mind, for whatever reason, was that of a farm. Having never been to the Greenhouse Garden Center before, it is a pleasant surprise when the duo pulls into the parking lot. After adventure earlier at the manor in the bushes, she is happy not to be walking around a muddy farm today. Zeus and Myrtle enter the Garden

Center where they receive a friendly greeting from a young bright-eyed employee named Lauren. "Welcome to the Greenhouse Garden Center, do you need help finding anything?" The Detective flashes his badge and introduces himself and Myrtle. Lauren appears nervous but is happy to answer whatever questions they have. Most people get unnerved when approached by the Police, so Myrtle did not hold it against her. Zeus has questions about what type of plants they carry, so Lauren shows them around the Greenhouse. She leads them to an outside display area where the overhead parallel wood beam trellises provide some shade, while still maintaining that outdoor feeling. "What would you like to see first, we have potted plants, hanging plants, perennials, annuals, tropical, evergreen, maybe roses?", Lauren looks right at Zeus when the says roses. If it was an attempt to sell him some roses, it did not work, he is unbothered. Myrtle asks if they have plants that could be poisonous to humans. "Oh sure", answers Lauren while leading them to another part of the nursery. This part of the center is designated for employees only. In this section, there are bushes with pink flowers called Nerium Oleander, commonly known as Oleander. Lauren explains that the Oleander is versatile and commonly used for borders and hedges, however it is most toxic. The next plant Lauren shows them is the Foxglove. Myrtle and Zeus immediately perked up. Foxglove is a common ornamental plant with bell-shaped flowers in varying shades of purple and white. Lauren warns these flowers are extremely toxic to the cardiovascular and gastrointestinal system in humans and animals. This purple and white coloring appears to be the same as the flowers discovered in Denise's salad. Myrtle opens a picture of the salad on her phone to compare and they look the same. She shows the picture on her phone to Lauren. The young employee cannot confirm one hundred percent that it is Foxglove, but it appears to be.

Myrtle is curious if any of their persons of interest have visited the Greenhouse Garden Center recently. Was Chef Crowder, or any other persons of interest recently shopping here for flowers? Zeus excuses himself to seek out the store manager to request the sale records or surveillance footage from the last month to see if anybody purchased the poisonous Foxglove plant. Myrtle peruses a nearby stack of magazines while waiting for Zeus to return. This edition of the magazine is dedicated to the best local flower gardens in Viewgrove. The gardening magazine features Mrs. Dubai's garden on the cover. Zeus Chaplin locates the store manager and makes his request, but he is informed she would be happy to help once he comes back with a warrant. Zeus tries to talk to her but there is no changing the store manager's mind. He has no problem filing for a warrant once he gets back to the station, but it means lost time and another trip to the Greenhouse Garden

Center. Myrtle has an idea before they leave, she pulls up another picture in her phone to show to Lauren. "Have you seen this person around here before?" Lauren looks at the picture of Chef Crowder. To Myrtle's disappointment, she does not recognize Chef Crowder. She suggests asking one of her other co-workers since she only works at the Garden Center part-time. Before they go looking for another employee, Myrtle shows Lauren a second picture. "Do you recognize the person in this picture?" She stares at the picture for a moment. "I haven't seen the lady upfront, but I've seen the lady sitting behind her shopping here recently." The picture is of Mrs. Dubai and the lady sitting behind her is Denise. Myrtle asks Lauren if she is sure, "You have seen this lady around here recently?" Lauren nods yes "Sometimes she was alone and sometimes she came with a man." Zeus and Myrtle both look at each other. Myrtle starts frantically flipping through her phone until she finally finds what she is looking for. Her heart beats a little faster as she shows Lauren the next picture. "Look carefully, is this the man she came here with?" Lauren looks and immediately breaks into a smile, "Not him, that's Jean Pierre, he works here."

CHAPTER 15

Myrtle and Zeus drive away from the Greenhouse
Garden Center feeling very confused. Zeus knew it
was a bit of a long shot even going to the
Greenhouse. Myrtle is feeling a little hurt because
Denise never mentioned any man in her life, maybe
they were not as close as she thought they were?
Denise could be a private person at times, she did not
like to talk about herself or her past. Myrtle suggests
to Zeus that a visit to Denise's home at the Liberty
Apartment complex may provide a better picture of
who she was. "Lauren from the Greenhouse had
assumed the man was Denise's boyfriend since they
appeared so comfortable with each other", adds
Myrtle. She is talking for a few more minutes when
she realizes Zeus is not paying attention to her. The
whole ride over to Denise's place, Zeus is fuming
over Jean Pierre failing to mention that he worked at

the Greenhouse Garden Center. He has half a mind to drive right back over to the apartment complex and pay Mr. Pierre another visit, only this time he is not leaving without all the facts. Myrtle can tell by the look on the Detective's face that he is preoccupied with something. She believes he wants to solve the case however she knows there is also pressure to close the case as soon as possible. Myrtle makes another attempt to spark up a conversation, "Funny note, while you were waiting for the manager I saw a stack of garden magazines by the information desk, and guess who was on the cover?" she waits for a few beats, "Go ahead, guess." Zeus is in no mood for guessing games and immediately gives up without hazarding a single guess. She teases him about giving up too easy before revealing it was Mrs. Dubai. "Can you see her going to the Greenhouse and having Jean Pierre sell her flowers?", asks Myrtle playfully. Zeus smiles at the thought and jokingly reminds her that wealthy people like Mrs. Dubai do not shop at the Greenhouse with the regular folks, they buy the whole business and have things shipped to their homes.

Myrtle is the first to Denise's apartment door and discovers the door is cracked open. "Hello, is anybody here?" When no reply comes, she looks back at Zeus for his assessment. He puts his finger to his lips to quiet Myrtle while motioning for her to get behind him. Detective Chaplin draws his weapon and announces himself, "VG Police!" Still no reply so he carefully enters the apartment. He makes his way through the apartment and clears every room while Myrtle waits nervously at the door. Peering through the doorway she can only see into the living room and not any further. The apartment has been turned upside down. Zeus appears a few minutes later with the all-clear and holsters his weapon. Myrtle steps through the shallow foyer and into the living room. It feels like somebody had only recently moved in or had cleared the room to paint. The only furnishings are a futon couch and a wooden coffee table. The living room walls are bare, with no artwork, and no pictures of her or any family members. Zeus interrupts Myrtle's thoughts to ask if she wants to accompany him to find the building manager. He advises her not to touch anything while he finds out if the manager is aware of the break-in or has seen anybody suspicious around. Myrtle is way too interested in exploring the apartment to go tracking down the manager. Lined up along the wall by every window is a series of flowerpots containing mature plants, Denise's place is full of flowerpots. Myrtle catches a glimpse of a price sticker on one of the flowerpots, it says it came from the Greenhouse Garden Center. Myrtle checks more of the pots, and the larger plants have faded price stickers like they have been there a while. However, there are two small plants with shiny new stickers, also from the Greenhouse Garden Center. So, Lauren was correct,

Denise had spent a lot of time at the Greenhouse Garden Center. If Lauren was right about Denise, perhaps she was right about this mystery boyfriend. Perhaps there is some evidence of this mystery man in the apartment.

The bedroom door creaks in protest as Myrtle pushes it open. The blinds are closed, and the room is dim and cool. She pauses in the doorway, it feels weird entering the bedroom, somehow different from being in the living room. A chill hit her body when she enters the bedroom, simply being in the room makes her feel closer to Denise. Myrtle takes a moment to have a private conversation with her friend. With what she feels is Denise's permission, Myrtle proceeds to search the room. She uses a pen from her purse, so she does not disturb any fingerprints. There nothing in the dresser drawers except undergarments and folded t-shirts. In the closet hung a few dresses and a coat. At the bottom of the closet, among the pairs of shoes, is a black backpack. Myrtle kneels in front of the closet and unzips the smaller front pocket. The only item inside is an unmarked orange bottle of pills. She unzips the main pouch of the backpack with her pen and discovers is it packed like an overnight bag. Inside the backpack are toiletries, a change of clothes, a passport, and some cash neatly packed inside. On the bottom of the backpack are a few 4x6 pictures. Using the cuff of her shirt sleeve to cover her fingers she grabs the pictures. One of the pictures even has Myrtle in it. What interested Myrtle the most is that there were no family pictures or pictures older than two years ago. She can hear Zeus returning to the apartment. Then came a sudden loud voice.

"Who are you, what are you doing here?!"

The loud male voice startles Myrtle so much she drops the pictures on the floor, this is not Zeus. Her head is racing, and her heart starts beating rapidly. With her back turned she is at a disadvantage. Her eyes race around the closet looking for something she can use to try to defend herself against a pending attack. The loud voice is now commanding her to turn around. Myrtle steels herself and turns around to face this intruder with a high heeled boot in her hand, cocked and ready to put an eye out. The man in the doorway is tall, has short brown hair, and an athletic build. She is suddenly face-to-face with the mystery boyfriend and possible murderer.

"What are you doing here Myrtle Jenson?!"

CHAPTER 16

A shocked Myrtle stands frozen, unable to compose an answer to the question she was just asked. A scared and confused look displayed on her face. How does this mystery man know her name? Is he the person that tried to kill her? Her mind races to match his face to anybody from her old cases. He does not look familiar, so how does he know her name? There is only one way out of the bedroom and that is going through him, would she be able to make it past him though? There is no weapon in his hand, did he plan to strangle her to death with his bare hands? Myrtle steps back to put as much distance between them as possible. If she tosses the shoe hard enough at his head, it could buy her enough time to push past him and escape outside for help. Just as she is about to make a move, Detective Zeus Chaplin steps around the corner with his weapon drawn.

"VG Police, freeze, hands where I can see them!"

The intruder immediately freezes and slowly raises his hands. Myrtle has never been so happy to see Zeus in her life. It appears the apartment manager is with him also. Detective Zeus calls out to Myrtle and asks if she is okay? She calls back that she is fine, just shook up. The mystery intruder still blocks the doorway and prevents her from joining Zeus in the other room. Zeus instructs the apartment manager to pat the intruder down for weapons while he covers him. The apartment manager wants no part of this and shrinks back into the background. The intruder insists he is a federal agent working on a case. "Hold on officer, give me a chance to explain, my identification is in my jacket!" A federal agent working a case in Viewgrove sounds suspicious to Zeus, surely, he would have been briefed on any active Federal cases. He instructs the man to keep his hands up and slowly take his identification out, and then kick it over to Myrtle while he covers him. She picks up the identification and reads it out to Zeus, and sure enough, it says The Federal Bureau of Investigation.

Detective Chaplin is skeptical of the stranger's credentials, he is concerned they may be fake. He handcuffs the stranger and places him in the back of the squad car while he calls it in to the precinct to verify the authenticity. While they wait on Zeus,

Myrtle asks the apartment manager to share any security surveillance footage from the past few days. The apartment manager is ashamed but admits somebody broke the camera fixated on this row of apartments two months ago, and he just has not replaced it yet. Myrtle was hoping to have video evidence of whoever broke into Denise's apartment. Somebody had to turn over all the furniture, whoever was here was looking for something. She goes back into the bedroom and picks the pictures off the floor to show to the apartment manager. He studies the pictures for a few minutes, but he cannot say for sure if he has seen any of the people pictured visit the apartment. There could have been a man, but he cannot be sure. Myrtle gets the impression the apartment manager does not want to get involved. Perhaps he feels he is already in enough trouble for the busted camera not being repaired, she cannot be sure, he mentioned the building owner is a real lion. All his answers seem to end in 'I don't know?' A frustrated Myrtle badgers him to help them with anything he can remember. The apartment manager finally has enough and heads for the door, "Look, I'm just the super, I don't own this complex, I'm sorry." Myrtle had never been to Denise's apartment before, they always agreed to meet out somewhere. She is tempted to start knocking on neighbors' doors and asking about the stranger. Her heart tells her to go for it, but her mind prevails. If this stranger is truly an FBI agent, she wants to be sure whatever she does is legal, so Zeus does not get in trouble.

The badge confirmation comes back as authentic, so Zeus uncuffs the stranger and allows him out of the back seat of the squad car. He begins to explain his actions, but the agent suddenly stops him. He overheard dispatch updating the Detective of his status. The agent's name is Alex Ortiz. The FBI does not seem to be aware that he is currently in Viewgrove, they list him as being on vacation. Agent Ortiz follows Zeus back into the apartment where Myrtle is waiting. Once inside he makes a formal introduction. "Have we met before Sir; I don't recall ever meeting you?" asks Myrtle. Agent Ortiz admits they have never met. Before he can begin to say anything else, Myrtle hits him with the question everybody wants to know.

"What are you doing here Agent Ortiz?"

Alex Ortiz proposes they help each other and exchange information. Zeus figures the Agent is only being so cooperative because he is on unofficial business. If this were a bureau sanctioned operation, the Agent would have commandeered the scene and ordered him to stand down. Detective Zeus agrees to Agent Alex's proposal, only if the FBI agent goes first. Agent Alex explains that he was working with Denise, he only knows Myrtle because Denise spoke of her and showed him a picture. "Denise was fond of you, I feel like I know you, can I call you MJ?"

Myrtle shakes her head no, "You can call me Ms. Jenson." The agent goes on to say he had not heard from Denise, she was not answering her phone, so he decided to stop by and check on her. He later learned why she was not answering her phone and he came by the apartment today looking for clues. Myrtle remembers going through Denise's cell phone records but does not recall seeing any calls to or from Alex Ortiz. When challenged about the phone calls, the Agent states he also called from a private number that would not show up on the phone records. Myrtle does not like the sound of this at all. What kind of boyfriend calls from a blocked phone line? "How long had you and Denise been dating?" Agent Alex responds in a tone that suggests he is forced to reveal something he does not want to.

"I'm not a boyfriend, Denise was in a witness protection program, and I was her handler."

CHAPTER 17

Denise was in witness protection. Denise was in witness protection? Myrtle does not believe what she is hearing, this guy must be lying but why. According to Agent Alex, he placed Denise in hiding in Viewgrove two years ago while awaiting a major trial date. There had been some recent chatter about the case, and he feared her location had been compromised. That is all he will say, he refuses to tell them what trial or the parties involved. At this point, he feels he has shared enough and wants to know why Zeus and Myrtle broke into Denise's apartment. He also seems to be under the impression they turned all the apartment furniture over, and wants to know what they were looking for? Myrtle's eyes widen, the nerve of this guy thinking they broke into the apartment. She cannot let that slide, as she likes to say, 'Once you let them slide, they want to start figure skating.' Agent Alex can tell by Myrtle's tone she is upset and immediately wishes he would have framed the question differently. She makes it very clear to him, in no uncertain terms, that she is not a burglar that goes around breaking into apartments. The door was open when they got there. She will do what it takes to find out who killed Denise and questions why the Agent assumes they must have broken in. The FBI agent appears taken aback and tries to assure Myrtle that he is not trying to racially profile them. Zeus also takes offense to the nature of the question, but he is much more diplomatic with his response. He assumes Agent Alex will be able to make a call and easily find out anyway. The Detective advises the FBI Agent that they are in the middle of a murder investigation and the clues led them to Denise's apartment. Agent Alex turns to leave but advises them both he will be verifying their story with the Viewgrove Police Department.

Myrtle and Zeus race back to the police station to research any big pending court cases. She offers to contact her friend at the local newspaper for assistance. Davina Roberts, at the Viewgrove Gazette has assisted Myrtle in the past on cases. Zeus advises against it, for now, the last thing this case needs is more publicity. If the press gets involved it would just complicate their investigation. There is already enough pressure to close the case from his boss as it is. This murder happened at a dinner event that was attended by a lot of prominent town people. They are not interested in a lengthy investigation. Quite honestly, they would prefer it to be officially labeled an accident and the case closed. Nobody in those circles wants to take a hit to their reputation by being linked to a murder investigation. A big public news story might send them over the deep end. Zeus has lived in town much longer than Myrtle has, so he has witnessed and experienced how quickly bad news travels around town. Viewgrove is still one of those towns where your reputation matters. Sitting unopened in the Detective's email box right now is a message from the young Police Commissioner requesting an update on the case. Zeus is not a fan of communicating through email, so he has not even bothered to look at it yet. He is from a different time and prefers face-to-face interactions and phone calls over emails and text messages. The Police Commissioner is the youngest to ever occupy the position and is trying to usher in a new modern error that takes advantage of the latest technology. After she took over, conference room meetings became video conference calls, and email became the preferred method of communication. Zeus checks his email at the last possible moment on purpose, it is a personal protest over the new changes. Whenever he gets questioned about his slow response time, he pretends not to know how to use the technology. The Technical Support department has sent a trainer to the Viewgrove station at least three times to try and teach Zeus how to use his computer.

The keyboard keys tap as Myrtle uses Zeus's desktop to search online for big-time cases from around two years ago. Zeus is on the phone with the FBI also trying to find more information about the case. The FBI confirms Alex Ortiz is an active Agent and they can account for his whereabouts on the night of Denise's death. Outside of eliminating their agent as a suspect, they are unwilling to cooperate. A Detective from a smaller town they have probably never heard of does not hold much weight with the Bureau. They place him on hold and talk in circles for half an hour. Zeus Chaplin finally slams the phone receiver down in frustration, it is loud enough to cause everybody nearby to look up. Myrtle has never seen him like this, usually, he is the calm and collected one, it was a little scary. Zeus blurts out, "I'm going for a coffee, you want one?" She does not know what to say, caffeine is probably the last thing he needs right now, but she was not going to be the one to tell him. She manages a mumbled no thank you and looks up in time to watch him walk off toward the breakroom.

It figures that as soon as Zeus walks away she would find something. She looks up to try and catch him before he gets too far but he is already out of view. Myrtle starts to get excited because this could be something, maybe it is true that the answers to everything are available on Google. This case she found would have been around the time she moved to Viewgrove. She is embarrassed to admit it but since she moved to town, she has become more concerned with local news and does not follow much of anything else. The news story is about a man that fell to his death through a glass ceiling two years ago. A police investigation concluded it was not an accident, as initially thought, but a murder. With the help of a star witness, the police were able to build a murder case against an organized crime boss. According to the article posted three days ago, the court date has finally arrived. Just then it hits her,

"Oh, my goodness, I wasn't the target."

CHAPTER 18

Detective Zeus Chaplin returns to his desk with his coffee only to find Myrtle Jenson staring at him with a funny look on her face. He does not know what her problem is, he asked her if she wanted a coffee before he left and she said no, she needs to fix her face. Myrtle shares her revelation with Zeus. Could it be all this time they have been looking at the case the wrong way? He is initially skeptical but must admit he has not found a connection between Myrtle and this case. The items from Denise's apartment are still being processed. The bottle of pills that were in Denise's backpack has been sent to the Laboratory for analysis. Zeus reviews the online newspaper stories about the case two years ago. It will need some additional verification, but it appears this is the case Agent Alex is talking about. Furthermore, the background search did not produce any results from longer than two years ago. There are no credit cards, bank statements, or even a library card more than a couple years old. It is as if Denise Washington did not exist until two years ago, before that she is a ghost. Zeus turns to Myrtle to ask a question he does not want to, "Was Denise an FBI agent or maybe a spy?" The question falls on deaf ears, Myrtle is too busy wondering how she missed all these things about Denise, there must have been clues. Denise may not have felt comfortable enough to confide in her, or maybe she was a spy. She is not so sure Agent Alex did not just double-cross and kill his partner for a reason not yet known to them. She knows Zeus was getting nowhere with the Federal Bureau, but she is still going to ask him to see if Denise was also an Agent, possibly working undercover. Detective Zeus is tired of chasing ghosts, he wants answers. The first person on his list to speak to is that waiter, Jean Pierre. The waiter worked at the Greenhouse Garden Center, maybe he saw Denise and the FBI agent there? Plus, Zeus wants an explanation for why he did not disclose he worked at the Greenhouse. He tosses the empty coffee cup into the nearby trash can like a basketball player shooting a jump shot, all net, "Come on Myrtle, we're going to get some answers."

The duo speeds toward the waiter's apartment in the police car with lights flashing. Once they arrive at the apartment, Zeus hops out and runs up the outdoor stairs to the second floor. Myrtle pulls herself out of the car gingerly. By the time she gets out, Detective Zeus is already knocking on the waiter's apartment door. She doubts that he is home, Jean Pierre is too smart to stick around the apartment after getting a visit from the police earlier. On second thought, she decides to sit back down in the air-conditioned police cruiser and wait, it is hot out there. Moments later the Detective gets back in the car, he looks at his passenger sitting comfortably and wonders to himself why she did not get out of the car. Myrtle knows she will probably hear about it later. "He isn't here", growls Zeus as he turns the key in the ignition. The only other places Myrtle knows to look for the waiter are the Weatherford Manor, where Chef Crowder is currently set up, and the Greenhouse Garden Center. She is not welcome back to the Weatherford Manor, a story she does not want to explain to Zeus right now, so she suggests checking the Greenhouse Garden Center first. "Maybe he picked up a shift at the Greenhouse?", suggests Myrtle. Zeus needs no words of encouragement from his passenger, he reverses out of the parking spot and exits the apartment complex. The onsite apartment supervisor peeks through the office window to see who is in the lot, sees the Detective's police lights flashing, and closes the blinds. He does not tangle with the police unless he is forced to. The next stop for Myrtle and Zeus is the Greenhouse Garden Center.

Zeus finds a parking space toward the back of the parking lot. It is a busy day at the Greenhouse Garden Center, most likely due to the warm weather. Myrtle and Zeus enter the business in search of the manager. On the way to the Customer Service Desk, Myrtle keeps an eye out for the employee who had been so helpful on their last visit. She cannot remember the girl's name and maybe it is the matching clothes, but all these young employees look the same to her. The Customer Service desk sends a page out and within minutes the store manager is on the handheld walkie asking Jean Pierre to report to the Service Desk. When there is no response the store manager sends out a general call to ask if anyone has seen Jean. An employee responds over the walkie that Jean is working curbside pickups and he was retrieving an order from the supply closet earlier. The manager leads Myrtle and Zeus back to the Industrial Chemical Supply closet, commonly known to employees as the ISC. The Greenhouse Garden Center has a few commercial clients who require chemicals more potent than regular household needs. Only certain employees are trained and allowed to fill these orders. The ISC closet has a security code number pad on it, so customers cannot accidentally access it. The manager punches the code, swings open the door, and Jean Pierre falls out onto the floor. He has his uniform on, a bag of fertilizer nearby on the floor, and a set of keys in his hand. The store manager screams which causes a small crowd to start to gather. The open door releases a strong chemical odor from the storage room. The fumes cause Myrtle and Zeus to start coughing as the fumes lightly singe their lungs. They cover their nose and mouth while stepping back for fresh air. The store manager also steps back while coughing and calls out to customers and employees to clear the area. The store manager cannot believe the irony, "This was Jean's last week, we have to let him go because his Visa is expiring." Zeus got on his radio and called 911. Myrtle's hunch is confirmed shortly after when Zeus cannot find a pulse. Jean Pierre is dead.

CHAPTER 19

Zeus begins CPR on Jean Pierre's body. Paramedics respond to an emergency call at the Greenhouse Garden Center. While waiting for paramedics, Myrtle grabs a box of painter's mask off a nearby shelf to cover her nose and mouth. With the mask on, she sticks her head into the Industrial Chemical Supply closet to observe the scene. She promised Zeus she would not touch anything. There is still a chemical odor but most of it has dissipated. The room is about eight feet by eight feet with metal shelves full of fertilizer lining the walls. There are some drums of pesticides on the floor, the room is a chemical stockpile. The latch on the inside of the door is not functional and one of the industrial fertilizer drums was not closed properly, so it was emitting a toxic odor. The odor is not lethal if you can open the door. However, with the inside latch broken Jean Pierre was trapped and slowly succumbed to the fumes. "What kind of James Bond Villain style deathtrap is this?", wonders Myrtle out loud. She will have to wait for the official autopsy results, but that is how it appears to her. The image of the body tumbling out of the room onto the floor is not something she will forget anytime soon. One of the barrels catches Myrtle's eye, there is something crudely scratched on the side of it. The letters spell out 'fairwell.' On the wall are posted warnings and safety rules for the room. The Greenhouse Garden Center has a sign-in sheet where employees mark down what inventory they remove from the room. Based on the sign-in sheet it appears Jean Pierre came in the closet to collect a bag of fertilizer. A small crowd starts to arrive and gather around as the news travels through the store. Myrtle can hear the word accident, over and over as new people join the small crowd and get updated on what happened. She tries to pay the manager for the box of painter's masks but is told to keep them. One of their strongest leads is now dead in an apparent workplace accident, if only they could have gotten there sooner. The paramedics arrive and take over the CPR from Zeus, but they are unable to revive Jean Pierre.

The Viewgrove Police Department will need to contact the owner of the store regarding what happened. Detective Zeus Chaplin asks the store manager for the business owner's name and number for his report. With everybody appearing to be preoccupied, Myrtle takes this opportunity to take a closer look at the body, she is particularly interested in the hands. Jean Pierre has working man hands; they are rough to the touch and there is dirt under his fingernails. Judging by the unevenness, he chewed his nails, no manicures here. There is nothing unusual about his left hand, minus a few scrapes and cuts, but on his right hand there are also specs of faded blue dye. "I've heard of a green thumb, but this is blue." As a young woman, Myrtle once tried to save money by dying her hair. She did not think she needed to wear the plastic gloves that came with the kit, she was not a child after all. It felt like she was super careful, and her hair color came out surprisingly well. The pride she initially felt faded when she noticed the black specs of dye on her palms and fingernails. "How's this possible?" she thought, "I was so careful." The dye was impossible to wash out, she remembers having to wait days for it to completely disappear. The lesson learned is no matter how careful you are things always have a way of getting out. According to a co-worker, Jean Pierre's car is in the parking lot. Myrtle would love the chance to search the car after the police have processed it. She walks up to Zeus to tell him about the blue dye, just then the store manager advises him the parent company for this location is Lionfish LLC. Her ears immediately perk up, where has she heard that name before. "Does the name Lionfish mean anything to you, Zeus?" She will not get any help from him; he is not familiar with the name. The store manager comes to the rescue though, "Oh, Lionfish LLC owns a lot of things around town, stores, apartment buildings, all kinds of stuff."

Why does that name Lionfish LLC sound so familiar? Wait, that is it! Myrtle goes flipping through the pictures in her phone gallery until she finds the ones from the Chef's office. Sure enough, in the desk drawer was a contract offer from a company by that same name. "Detective, we need to find out who owns the Lionfish LLC?" Now does not seem to her like a good time to admit to breaking into Chef Crowder's office, maybe later. Zeus leaves the other officers to wrap up the scene and then returns to Myrtle. "Okay, what's up, why are you so interested in who owns Lionfish LLC?" She finally must come clean about breaking into Chef Crowder's office, and about the contract she found. Myrtle apologizes and even tries to offset the bad news by including the discovery of the blue dye on Jean Pierre's hand. She braces herself for the huge lecture, but nothing comes. Zeus is irritated but all he does is turn and walk out to the car. She is not sure if she should follow him, but he is her ride. He is quiet as she follows him out to the car. The Detective gets on the radio and asks for whomever is on duty to find out who owns the Lionfish LLC. They both wait in silence, neither one of them making eye contact with the other. The officer comes back on the radio with the search results. It turns out the Lionfish LLC is listed as the owner of record on a few properties including the Greenhouse Garden Center, and the Liberty Apartment complex. Zeus recalls the complex that Denise was living in was named the Liberty Apartment complex, he makes eye contact with Myrtle and she already knows it. The officer states it took some digging through a few shell corporations, but the Lionfish LLC is owned by Mrs. Fannie Dubai. The Detective shuts off the radio and turns to face Myrtle. "I keep asking you to follow procedures, but you continue to disregard them, I'm driving you back home now, you're off this case."

CHAPTER 20

The ride back to Myrtle's home is a quiet one. She knows some of her actions have the potential to compromise the case and put Zeus in a bad spot with his superior officers. Her goal was to find out who killed her friend, this case was personal to her. She was willing to do whatever she thought was necessary with little regard for whom her actions may affect. Myrtle has pushed the limits on the rules on other cases, but she has done it this time and her partner has had enough. She is terribly sorry for the position she has put her friend Detective Zeus in and accepts his decision to take her off the case. Sitting around her apartment gives her too much time with her thoughts. For a distraction, Myrtle decides to head out to Anna's Diner to drown her sorrows in turtle sundae. It is hard not to feel better after a dish of vanilla ice cream covered in hot caramel, rich fudge, pecans, topped with whipped cream and cherries. She first started coming to Anna's Diner for the Butter Pecan ice cream, two scoops in a waffle cone placed in a cup. Other places around town have good ice-cream and frozen yogurt but she likes this place the best. Plus, the diner has a big picture window that faces the busy Sunset Auditorium, so it is a great place to people-watch from. Most people order their ice-cream orders to go, so the Diner is never crowded and makes a great place to sit and be alone with your thoughts. All Myrtle can think about is the case, she cannot help but replay everything over and over in her head. Maybe she can talk to Zeus and try to make it up to him once he cools off. For now, she plans to just give him some space. A wise person once told her to never cut what you can untie. He has taught her so much in the short time they have worked together. Her friendship with him is important to her and she would hate for it to end over something like this. She will call him in the morning and try to make things right between them.

Meanwhile, back at the Viewgrove police station, the investigation continues. Zeus pays Janna the Medical Examiner a visit. Janna is always happy to receive a visit from the Detective, she enjoys teasing him. He is one of the few people that talks to her like a person so he will always be welcome there for as long as she is the Medical Examiner. Plus, he is the only one she can get to drink her home-grown coffee.

The rumor around the department is she fertilizes her coffee bean soil with human bits from the morgue, but Zeus does not believe any of that. Janna greets her guest with a warm welcome, "Zeus, good to see you, where's your girlfriend?" The Detective explains that it is just him today. Janna does not even care to ask a follow-up question. She likes it better without Myrtle around anyway, she thinks Ms. Jenson is weird. Detective Chaplin turns down the cup of coffee offered by Janna. When he declines to share a cup of coffee, she figures this is not a social call. Zeus requests the results of the analysis of the bottle of unknown pills. The request for analysis came into the Medical Examiner's office as a rush and if there is one thing Janna hates it is a rush request. "Oh, so you're the one who ordered the rush!" She walks over to one of the drawers and retrieves a printout. The mystery pills found in Denise's backpack are Benzodiazepines, commonly used for their sedating effects. The Medical Examiner cannot trace where the pills came from, however, she can confirm there were no Benzodiazepines in Denise's system when she died. Zeus assumes the medicine bottle is missing a label because Denise Washington was an alias, she either transferred the bottle or maybe her handler Agent Alex acquired them for her. They only found one bottle of pills and coupled with the fact there were no traces in her system perhaps she only used them recreationally.

The Medical Examiner confirms the dye on Jean Pierre's hand is a match for the dye in Denise's salad. Moments earlier Zeus had learned the waiter's fingerprint also matched prints pulled from the salad plate. Matching prints were also found on the refrigerators, ice machine, and food preparation tables. All this places Jean Pierre at the scene of the crime. It appears they have the correct man. Once the Detective's superiors learn about the dye and fingerprint match there will be a lot of pressure on him. There will be an immediate call from the Police Chief and the Mayor to charge Jean Pierre with murder and close the case. From the beginning, the Mayor has been calling for a swift, and discreet investigation. Professor Weatherford's attorney has threatened to sue the Police Department over the handling of the case. Zeus technically has everything he needs to officially file this case away so why does it not feel right. He should be happy to be rid of this case, he knows his supervisors will be extremely excited to put a lid on this one. For one thing, he is missing a motive. Why would Jean Pierre want to kill Denise? It does not make any sense. He could close the case, and nobody would care if there was no clear motive. Life would go on, he would work the next case, and perhaps even receive an award for solving the case. Life would seem great, but he would know, he would always know. Detective Zeus has never closed a case just to meet a quota, and now that he is in the twilight of his career, he is not about to start.

He decides he must keep the case open and accept any consequences that come because of that decision. If the Police Department fires him and closes the case his conscious will be clear knowing he tried to do the right thing. Detective Zeus Chaplin knows what he must do. He gathers himself, pulls out his flip phone, and dials the saved number. He places the phone to his ear, while unsure he would get an answer, he listens to it ringing. The phone rings a few times with no answer, he will give it a few more seconds before he hangs up.

"Hello, this is Myrtle."

CHAPTER 21

The two friends share what is initially an awkward conversation. Myrtle does not waste any time before apologizing for jeopardizing the case. Zeus had already forgiven her 30 seconds into their conversation. She will never know it, but he has a smile on his face as soon as she picked up the phone. It is as Myrtle likes to say, what is understood does not have to be explained. He knows she is sorry about the whole thing. This case hits close to home and if it were him, who is to say he would not take every opportunity to find evidence. The truth is they make a great team. Myrtle pushes Zeus to think outside of the box, and Zeus provides her with some structure. Zeus has never worked with anybody like her before, and although she is not an officer, he considers her a partner. There are more than a few criminal cases in Viewgrove that would have gone unsolved if it were not for her. He is continuously trying to educate her on police procedure. She does not know it, but he is ultimately trying to prepare her to be able to work police cases without him. Zeus does not plan on doing this work forever. The older he gets, the more time he finds himself thinking about the future. Ten years ago, he would have caught up to the waiter before he had a chance to make it to the opposite staircase. This job used to be everything to him, but it no longer feels that way. Zeus has not shared this with anybody, but he has been contemplating retirement. He has enough time spent on the job to receive a decent pension. Viewgrove is not the sleepy town it was when he first arrived there, while not at the level of some big metropolises, the crime is getting worse. His daughter has been trying to get him to retire and move back to the big city with her. Zeus would feel better about leaving if he knew Myrtle was here to help keep Viewgrove safe.

So here Zeus is with now two deaths on his hands. How is he expected to solve these cases when the suspects keep dying? Speaking of suspects, are there any suspects in the waiter's death or is this truly an accident. He often looks up across the police station floor and realizes most of the other officers are half his age, some are young enough to be his kids. He wonders where the time went. There is no time to think about that now. It is a good thing he reinstated Myrtle because he will need some help with these cases. Myrtle agrees to meet Zeus at the Police Station. He is glad to see her walk through the door, now he is not the only senior in the room. The two immediately get to work. Myrtle has questions about the waiter's death being an accident. Just as they were closing in on the killer, the waiter turns up dead, it just seems too convenient. She pulls up the Consumer Reports on the type of lock that is installed on the Greenhouse Garden Center supply closet door. The door lock scores high marks for dependability. She cannot find any complaints anywhere online about the lock malfunctioning. The Greenhouse reps have hinted they may be looking into suing the lock manufacturer. However, by all indications, the lock is reliable with a good rating. Myrtle and Zeus both examined the lock and agreed it did not appear to be old or in disrepair. This leads Myrtle to believe the lock was tampered with to cause it to malfunction and trap Jean Pierre inside that storage closet. Zeus does not have a reasonable explanation for why the lock malfunctioned, just poor luck perhaps. Myrtle calls the Greenhouse Garden Center manager to ask her how often people go into that supply closet. The Greenhouse manager is surprised to be getting a call, but advises the supply closet is only accessed when a commercial order is placed for pick up. Due to the dangerous chemicals in that closet, the company tries to minimize the amount of contact the employees have. An additional safety step the Greenhouse takes is to only assign access to specially trained employees.

Myrtle figures if somebody did murder Jean Pierre, they would need to know he was one of the employees trained to access that supply closet, the days he worked, and the times to assure he would be the one accessing the supply closet.

Myrtle asks Zeus, "How about Chef Crowder, would he have a reason to kill Jean Pierre?" Zeus admittingly does not follow her line of thought. He cannot think of any reason why the Chef would want to kill the waiter. Speaking of motive, the Detective cannot think why the waiter, Jean Pierre, would murder Denise Washington either. Zeus disagrees, "I can't think of any reason the Chef would want to kill the waiter." He feels the waiter was just randomly employed by the Chef that night. Jean Pierre was picked out of a line up sent by the Let's Eat Catering Company. Myrtle asks if there is any way to detain Chef Crowder and prevent him from leaving town. Maybe if they interviewed him again, he would slip up and reveal his connection to either murder. Myrtle is not a big believer in coincidences, so she is looking for a link between the two murders. Both murders, assuming Jean Pierre was murdered, were well executed, and designed to appear like accidents. In each instance, there is no security footage capturing the suspects. These murders were not committed by amateurs, the crime scenes were wiped clean, the job of well-financed professionals. The only thing Myrtle has to go on is a few eyewitness reports of strangers or tourists in suits around town. In a tourist town like Viewgrove that is not much to go on. This could easily be a case of people watching too many mobster movies. Myrtle reviewed the footage from the Greenhouse Garden Center security cameras. The footage did not capture any mobsters on or around the premises, however it did capture a delivery van pulling into the loading zone of the parking lot. The curious thing to her is nobody gets in or out of the van, and nobody ever came out to the van. The delivery van parks for around ten minutes before driving away. Myrtle can barely make out the badging on the side of the van, is it a type of animal?

CHAPTER 22

A buzz starts to circulate the precinct that the Weatherford Manor case has been solved. Officers are still hearing the news and stopping by the Detective's desk to congratulate him. At that moment Zeus is glad Myrtle is back and is embarrassed to explain why co-workers are stopping by to congratulate him. If this keeps up, he expects to begin receiving calls from the local press soon. Myrtle is glad to be back on the case and does not care about what else is going on. She is not even going to give him a hard time about all the extra attention. The investigation board is still set up, Zeus could not bring himself to take it down yet. The board shows pictures of the possible suspects along with corresponding evidence. Myrtle has had a chance to step back from this case for a moment. She hopes it allows her to see something with fresh eyes she may have missed before. She walks up to the investigation board and goes over what they know.

Denise Washington:

Denise Washington is an alias. Everything the police can find appears to support this. It appears she was involved in a big FBI murder case a few years ago. She witnessed something she should not have. Denise's mystery boyfriend turns out to be her handler. He relocated her with a new identity to Viewgrove two years ago to keep her safe so she could testify later. She was nervous and took pills for anxiety, possibly over the upcoming trial. Her apartment was turned upside down.

Agent Alex Ortiz:

Agent Alex is with the FBI. He placed Denise in Viewgrove as part of the witness protection program and was supposed to keep her safe. He failed. He had returned to Viewgrove to retrieve her to testify in the big murder case only she was killed before he could deliver her back. Looks like the Greenhouse Garden Center was one of the places Denise liked to meet the FBI agent.

Mrs. Fannie Dubai:

The Greenhouse Garden Center is owned by Lionfish LLC, which is owned by Mrs. Fannie Dubai. Mrs. Dubai owns lots of businesses in town. Her reputation is that she does big business deals, but not always with the most reputable business partners. The Viewgrove Police have several reports filed with the Better Business Bureau about her business practices, but there have been no convictions. The complaints include blackmail, extortion, and espionage. The waiter worked at the Greenhouse.

Chef Crowder:

Had a contract in his desk from Lionfish LLC. Mrs. Fannie Dubai may be trying to take over Chef Crowder and his business. Myrtle is not a lawyer, but the contract appears to transfer the controlling interest of his company. It is rumored that he committed insurance fraud when one of his restaurants suspiciously burned down. The Viewgrove Police Department's research shows the investigation was dropped due to a lack of conclusive evidence. He hired the waiter to work at the event.

Jean Pierre (Waiter):

He worked as a waiter at the party that night and served the deadly salad. He had access to the poisonous flower because he also worked at the Greenhouse Garden Center. Viewgrove Police Department research uncovers he is in the country on an expired Visa. His application for a green card has been denied. He was facing deportation. In his car, the police found a packed bag and a large sum of cash. He appears to have committed the murder. What was his motivation? He had a stack of money so why show up for work at the Greenhouse and risk getting picked up for possible deportation?

Myrtle scowls at the evidence board trying to figure out what they are missing. Suddenly that scowl turns into a wide smile, she has it. Zeus recognizes that smile, "You solved it didn't you?" Myrtle needs to check one thing out, but she is quite sure she knows who did it. She points to the picture of Jean Pierre's crime scene, more specifically the picture of the drum with the letter scratched in on it. Zeus looks at the drum, "What, his goodbye note? He didn't even spell it right." Myrtle taps on the picture of the barrel, "I don't think this is a case of poor spelling, I think he was trying to tell us something." She explains that the waiter used his keys to scratch a note before he died. The laboratory analysis confirms paint chips matching the barrel were found on the keys. Next, she highlights the picture of the keys. Zeus agrees those keys were used to scratch the letters but why is that important. Myrtle points at the picture of the keyring, "These aren't workplace keys, these are his home keys, I remember them from when we were at his apartment." She poses a question, "Jean Pierre was a renter, how many keys would he have?" Zeus guesses maybe 3. Myrtle checks the report and points out that they know what every key on Jean Pierre's key chain unlocks except for one. The Detective swings around to retrieve the evidence bag with the keyring. Myrtle does not recognize the key, but Zeus does, he has lived in town longer. He was there when they first built the train station, and he used to see lots of these keys. He remembers years ago it used to be popular for teenagers to hide their drugs from their parents in these lockers. Myrtle smiles, "We call it VG Station but what's the official name of the train station?" A smile now creeps over his face too, "Thomas Fairwell Train Station!"

Zeus Chaplin dispatches two officers to the train station to retrieve the contents of the locker. Just as Myrtle predicted, the extra key on Jean Pierre's keyring fits a locker in the station. The officer turns the key and opens the locker to reveal nothing, the locker is empty. He radios back to Detective Chaplin to tell him the locker is empty. Myrtle is convinced she is right and asks him to feel around the locker for a false bottom, hidden panel, or something. The officer radios back, sure enough, there is a thumb drive taped to the ceiling of the locker.

"Once we learn what is in that locker, we will learn who our killer is", advises Myrtle.

The officers return promptly to the Police station with the thumb drive. Myrtle cannot wait to see what is on it, but she must play it cool to not tip off anybody in the office. This case is supposed to be closed after all. Zeus inserts the thumb drive into his desktop and a short list of files opens. Myrtle had a hunch, but she was still surprised to see how much information was in the files on this thumb drive. It was Jean Pierre speaking to them from the grave, and he wanted somebody to know exactly who was responsible in the event of his death. To keep such evidence hidden away he must have known what this person was capable of. Myrtle and Zeus are glued to the screen in anticipation of what information is stored on the memory stick. There are only three items on the memory stick, a letter the waiter wrote, a screen print of a financial news website, and a picture. They pour over the information in part confusion and part amazement. Zeus still wants to keep this new evidence between the two of them, so he toggles between screens on his computer monitor every time someone comes by to congratulate him on the case. Myrtle is impressed because she does not know how to do that. Every year she tells herself she is going to learn how to use the computer better and every year she does not. Myrtle has one last request of the officers she trusts. She sends the officer on a short errand to the local pawn shop, and she is to call back to the station with her findings right away. The next thirty minutes are spent pacing around the police station while waiting for the officer to call. The phone finally rings, hello, a wry smile creeps across her face because it is just as she expected.

CHAPTER 23

Upon arrival, they push the buzzer on the speaker box. "Yes, can we help you", crackles a voice through the speaker box. Myrtle yells from the passenger seat, "Myrtle Jenson and Detective Chaplin to see Mrs. Fannie Dubai." The speaker box crackles, "Enter once the gate is open." The gate buzzes and slowly begins to open and allow them access to the driveway. Myrtle and Zeus taxi up the driveway to the house. They knock and the butler answers the door immediately, he must have been waiting at the door to welcome them. He lets them inside, but not before he announces them. Mrs. Dubai is already aware; she has been watching her uninvited guests drive up the driveway on the security camera. Myrtle has been inside the home before, and it is just as impressive as the first time she saw it. The look on Zeus's face says he is impressed as well, the grand staircase, dark wooden accents, painted portraits on the wall, and the vaulted ceilings that seem to go on forever. The two guests are led past the impressive cylindrical salt-water aquarium, Myrtle fights the urge to point out all the amazing things to Zeus as they walk past them. She has so many more questions for the butler about the décor and paintings on the wall, but she does not want to disappoint Zeus again. The butler leads them into a parlor where Mrs. Fannie Dubai is waiting. The hostess rises to her feet to greet her guests. As usual, she is dressed like she is going to an award show. Her makeup is fully done, she is wearing a designer gown, and sporting her customary jewelry. "MJ, so good to see you again, and who's your boyfriend?" Myrtle is quick to correct her host, "Call me Ms. Jenson. This is Detective Zeus Chaplin from the Viewgrove PD." Mrs. Dubai apologizes to Myrtle and Zeus for calling him her boyfriend. "Charles will be back in a moment with some refreshments, how do you take your coffee Detective?"

Fannie Dubai does not seem bothered by their presence at all, it almost feels like she is happy to have the company. Detective Zeus declines the coffee offer and advises his host of the nature of the visit. "No thank you, it's not a social call, we're here to talk to you about the Denise Washington case." Just then Charles the butler walks in with a silver tray of coffee and muffins. It did not go unnoticed that on the tray was artificial sweetener and half-and-half creamer, this lady is good. Myrtle is so tempted to at least sample the icing glazed cinnamon cobbler muffins, and 'see how-they-eat' as she likes to say. Fannie pours herself a cup of coffee before she responds to the Detective.

"That was a terrible accident, I didn't know the lady, it was so sad."

Zeus asks Mrs. Dubai if she knew the waiter Jean Pierre. Fannie states she does not know who that is either. "Pierre? It's so hard to keep up these days. Is he or she one of those YouTube stars the kids are raving about now?", she asks while casually taking a bite out of her muffin. Myrtle steps in to set the scene. "I believe you know exactly who both Denise Washington and Jean Pierre are, the two cases are connected." She begins to paint the picture for both the Detective and Mrs. Dubai. "You hired John Pierre to poison Denise Washington in exchange for securing him a green card and avoiding deportation." Fannie does not even flinch after hearing that accusation. She sits in her seat calmly enjoying her pastry as if she were listening to the weather forecast for the week. Did she think she was untouchable? "Mrs. Dubai, one of the arenas you love to indulge in is information, you're obsessed with it. You use it for leverage in your business dealings and probably trade it or do favors to close business deals, and I think that is what happened here." Myrtle goes on to describe how she suspects Mrs. Dubai was in negotiations for a huge business deal with some less than honorable characters. In exchange they wanted a star witness in an upcoming court case eliminated. "I'm thinking there must have been major dollars involved for you to go this far. You knew where Denise lived, your company Lionfish LLC owns the complex. Your new business partners are most likely responsible for trashing her apartment while looking for any shreds of evidence she might have hidden there."

Mrs. Dubai is not impressed. "Oh wow, that is an amazing made-up story, you should be writing murder mystery books like that lady on that old television show!" Myrtle speculates that Fannie Dubai most likely chose Jean Pierre because she had some leverage over him, due to being his employer at the Greenhouse and knowing his Visa status. Once Denise's death was upgraded to murder, it complicated things. The investigation delayed him getting paid and probably delayed any work on his green card application. This way it ensured he stayed around town, and if everything fell completely apart, he could always be blamed for everything. It turns out Jean Pierre was not as naïve as she had hoped, and he left some evidence in the event something happened to him. Some cash was found in Jean Pierre's car. She explains that the thumb drive contains a letter where he apologizes to the victim's family and lays out his agreement with Mrs. Dubai. The screenshot is of a financial news website that was running a story on how a certain crime family was still making major business deals while awaiting trial. The trial date is finally coming up, so Denise would have been required to testify, it is the reason Agent Ortiz is in town. In Myrtle's eyes, Fannie Dubai has motive and opportunity. "That is an extravagant story Ms. Jenson, you have a very vivid imagination, my lawyers will tear your case apart", states Fannie before asking, "Where is your proof?" Mrs. Dubai calmly pours herself another cup of coffee. "Ahh, Mrs. Dubai, but I do have proof, you're wearing it." Zeus is anxious to see what happens next, his whole case is on the line. Myrtle continues her story and explains that the third thing on the thumb drive is a picture of a hand wearing a ring. The hand has been confirmed as Jean Pierre's. When Jean Pierre's body was found he was not wearing a ring. His car and apartment were searched but there was no ring found. An officer today paid a visit to the local pawnshop and the owner identified Jean Pierre as the person who came in to have the ring appraised. Myrtle states she believes Mrs. Dubai could not have that ring showing up in a pawn shop. She estimates the ring was given to Jean Pierre to hold as collateral on his payment. "You are well connected around town, I'm sure you learned about the visit to the pawnshop. The waiter needed cash to leave town." She believes Fannie got her ring back in exchange for the cash that was found in the waiter's car. Myrtle produces a picture of the ring. "I looked at all of the pictures taken of you that night and something is missing, the photographer did a fantastic job, you're going to love how the pictures came out." Mrs. Dubai cuts in, "I always look good in pictures, Is there a point to this story?" Myrtle continues with her thought, "I've looked at every picture of you I could find on the internet, and in each picture, you are wearing a ring, the same ring Jean Pierre is wearing in this picture, the same ring you have on your finger now." Now Myrtle leans in, "How are you wearing a ring that Jean Pierre had in his possession earlier today? If we swab that ring, I'm sure we will find his fingerprints and DNA all over the ring." Myrtle is not done, "So you see, once we start investigating you, a lot of the missing pieces will fall into place, and we'll find out whom you got to sabotage that door lock at the Greenhouse and kill Jean Pierre as well. Go ahead and arrest her Detective." Mrs. Dubai sets her coffee cup back on the serving tray, "You may as well help yourselves to the refreshments before we go, there is no reason to waste a perfectly good pot of Jamaican Blue Mountain coffee." Detective Zeus rises to address Fannie Dubai, "You are under arrest for suspicion of murder. You have the right to remain silent. Anything you say can and will be used against you in a court of law. You have the right to talk to an attorney and have them present while you're being questioned. If you cannot afford an attorney, one will be appointed to represent you."

CHAPTER 24

Once Mrs. Dubai has been taken into police custody, Zeus has a few questions for Myrtle. "What gave it away, how did you know she was the one?" Myrtle explains the case turned when she realized she was not the target and Denise was. She had gone over the evidence several times in her mind but come up with nothing. Something Detective Zeus said earlier stuck in her mind. People like Fannie Dubai do not get their hands dirty; they go out and get other people to do things for them. When she first met Mrs. Dubai, she boasted about how she knew exactly who would be sitting next to her ahead of time. Information and the leverage that it affords her is her business. There are several complaints on file with the Better Business Bureau about her business practices. There are probably several complaints that have not been filed. "What led you to the Greenhouse Garden Center?" Myrtle explains how under questioning, Jean Pierre tried to make it seem like the flowers could have come from any number of places around town. He could have said nursery or garden center, but he mentioned the Greenhouse. The Lionfish company name kept appearing. Myrtle believes they met somewhere neutral and Jean Pierre asked for the ring as collateral upfront, he knew it was something she would not want to just part with. Once an investigation was opened, she asked him to wait and lay low. Worst case, she could use him as a scape goat. "I did a google image search on that van on the security camera footage, turns out the logo was a Lionfish and not an animal."

The way Myrtle figures it, Jean Pierre had nothing to lose, and at some point, became the right type of desperate. If he were to be deported it would cost him everything. Unless you have been in that situation, who knows what you would do to avoid deportation. Working at the Greenhouse Garden Center gave Jean Pierre access to the poisonous flower. Working for Chef Crowder that evening gave him access to Denise. Jean Pierre was handpicked by Fannie Dubai. Zeus asks a question, "How did Mrs. Dubai know Jean Pierre would be working the event?" Myrtle loves good questions; she has always heard there are no such things as bad questions, but she does not believe that. Her motto has always been If you are going to be stupid, then be quiet too. Ms. Jenson explains how Fannie Dubai planted Jean

Pierre on the scene. She had leverage over Chef Crowder. Enough leverage to compel the Chef to pick Jean Pierre out of the applicants the catering company sent over. Myrtle examined Mr. Pierre's hands after he died, and they were a workman's hands. She would describe them as rough, and judging by the unevenness she would guess he chewed his nails. Chef Crowder is so particular about whom he hires to work his events it is unlikely he would choose Jean Pierre based on the condition of his hands. Myrtle is no fan of the Chef, but she must admit he keeps his kitchen immaculate. There is just no way those dirty fingernails would be allowed to touch anything in that kitchen. The documents she found in the Chef's desk drawer from Lionfish LLC prove a connection to Fannie Dubai. If a lawyer were to examine the documents, she is sure it would show the Chef was fighting Lionfish LLC for control of his business. In the wild, the lionfish is considered an invasive species that attacks with poisonous spines when threatened, the same could be said to describe Mrs. Dubai. Myrtle asks Zeus if Chef Crowder could be charged as an accomplice. Zeus reminds her that the Chef may not have known the reason he was being asked to add the waiter to his staff for that night. He may have been told she was just helping a friend get a job. Myrtle is led to believe the Chef knew something because he pointed them in the waiter's direction when he gave Zeus that envelope with Jean Pierre's name on it. He also failed to mention that he was forced into hiring Jean Pierre. Zeus still wonders whatever became of that jacket. Myrtle believes the waiter must have disposed of it somewhere before they caught up to him. Now that he is dead, they will never know.

Myrtle thinks about how Mrs. Dubai almost got away with everything. Denise was unknown in town. By her design, she was a stranger with few friends. Mrs. Dubai was banking on the fact Denise had no family in town to raise a big fuss if she was in an accident. Myrtle thinks back on how it all started when Denise felt the heart attack, and while reaching for the glass of water on the table but ended up spilling it. Water spilled everywhere including the salad and mixed with the salad dressing causing the blue dye to come off the flowers. If not for that, her death would have been categorized as an unfortunate accident. "The person whom we think is the villain is working for a bigger villain", mumbles Zeus almost to himself as he shakes his head. Agent Ortiz is going to add these latest events to the charges on the upcoming court case. He vows to get justice. "This case just goes to show you, everyone has three lives, one public, one private, and one secret", adds Myrtle. "So, what happens now Detective?" she asks. Zeus's answer is a simple one, "Well, Agent Ortiz will try to get Mrs. Dubai to turn witness on whomever her business deal was with." Myrtle knows sometimes in these types of situations the FBI will make a deal with a lower level crook to catch a larger crook. This was a case of ugly greed. At this point, the case is out of her hands. "Quiet faith will bring you boundless rewards." She only hopes everyone involved with this murder gets all the jail time they deserve. Seeing Mrs. Dubai convicted and sentenced would do wonders for Myrtle's faith in the justice system. Due to the name Dubai being involved, the whole town of Viewgrove will be following the outcome of this case very closely, whenever it goes to trial.

CHAPTER 25

Detective Zeus Chaplin is still unable to locate any of Denise's family, to which nobody is surprised considering she was in the witness protection program. The FBI will not release that information to the Viewgrove Police Department. The FBI did claim the body and Myrtle can only hope they will return her to her home to be laid to rest. She hopes they inform the woman she knew as Denise's family so they will know what became of her. Myrtle takes it upon herself to post a short obituary in the Viewgrove Gazette to recognize Denise's time in town. Her friend Davina Roberts from the Gazette helps her to pull it together. She knows that Denise Washington was just an alias, but the person she met was real. The person she met was smart, kind, and thoughtful. It did not seem right not to do anything, so she decides to hold a small visual to honor her friend, and also give the people who knew her in town a chance to say goodbye. There is not a body to view, but people are free to share stories about the Denise they knew. Davina Roberts surprises Myrtle by creating a small memorial flyer to hand out to friends of Denise to mark the day. On the front are the date and Denise Washington's name. On the inside are a few pictures of Denise in happier times. On the back is printed some inspiration about seizing the day. It is a piece entitled 'Before the Day Ends.'

Myrtle opens the service to anybody who wants to say a few words. After a few people have spoken, she steps up and shares a few words about her friend Denise and what she meant to her. She closes by reading the poem on the back of the memorial flyer. The poem is dedicated to Denise but is also for her friends. Myrtle is by no means a poet, and this death feels senseless, but she wants to leave those in attendance with a message of hope.

Before the day ends,

Sing that song that's deep in your heart,

Before the day ends,

Forgive yourself for the times you weren't smart.

Before the day ends,

Be kind to a total stranger,

Before the day ends,

Pray your loved ones stay out of danger.

Before the day ends,

Smile your biggest smile so big and wide,

Before the day ends,

Breathe in the fresh air, you're blessed to be alive.

Before the day ends,

Reach out to whom you haven't spoken to in a while

Before the day ends,

Perform an act of kindness, make someone smile.

Before the day ends,

Take a moment to appreciate,

Before the day ends,

Give thanks for everything that makes this life great.

The visual was touching and after it was over everybody mingled for a little while before leaving to go their separate ways. Detective Zeus Chaplin and even Agent Ortiz stopped by the visual to pay their respects. Myrtle was grateful to see them both.

Earlier that day, before the funeral, Zeus received an award for outstanding detective work. Myrtle was in attendance, she thought he looked nice in his full uniform. She chuckled to herself when his name was called, she is so used to calling him Zeus, who is Casper Chaplin? She took some pictures of the ceremony for him to send to his daughter. His daughter and granddaughter live on the opposite coast and were unable to make it to the award ceremony. Zeus went from being on the verge of being suspended to receiving an award from the Police Commissioner for solving the case. The Detective believes it was just a chance for the Commissioner to get his name in the paper and maybe gain some national celebrity, and maybe favor at the FBI. Detective Chaplin does not do this work for the praise and awards, but he is deserving. In Myrtle's opinion, doing something you love is a fortunate way to live. After the ceremony, Zeus provides his crime-solving partner with an update on the case he received earlier. The police were finally able to interview Mr. Dubai, and he advised them he gave that ring to his wife as a wedding present years ago, it has her initials in the design making it one of a kind. Myrtle feels now that the case is solved, she should treat Zeus to a celebratory dinner. He was just given an award, plus it would be a good way to apologize to him for her actions on the case. "How about some Steak and Kidney pudding or Cottage Pie, what do you say Zeus?" He looks over at her and replies, "Only if you throw in some Bucatini served with peppercorn, sage, pecorino Romano, and truffle butter." Myrtle cannot help but laugh. Zeus is truly a class act and she is so relieved that they emerged from this case with their friendship intact. Doing this job without him would not be the same. It would be hard for him to admit it, but Zeus feels doing this job without Myrtle around would not nearly be as much fun either. After this case, the Detective is in no mood for any of that fancy gourmet food. "How about burgers and shakes at Anna's Diner?" Myrtle cracks a wry smile, she is starving, she thought he would never ask.

"Detective, turn on the lights so we can cut through rush hour traffic."

"Now, you know those are just for police business, but what the heck, just this once."

The squad car lights flash as Myrtle and Zeus head toward the Diner. At that moment Myrtle is reminded of something she heard once, 'You're only given this moment, if it makes you happy, I won't judge you.' Years later Myrtle came across that missing waiter's jacket in a Goodwill Store, it was cleaned, pressed, and ready for a new owner.

ABOUT THE AUTHOR

M. Malenga is an independent writer who lives and works in the United States. He is the author of Riddle of Darkness: A Myrtle Jenson Mystery and I Lied to you about Everything: A Myrtle Jenson Mystery. His advice for writers young and old is to keep writing. "Just because you don't know how doesn't mean it can't be done." ~ Judge Lynn Toler